# Sweet Hope

# Sweet Hope

**A NOVELLA**

**JUDSON N. HOUT**

Parkhurst Brothers, Inc.

LITTLE ROCK

**www.parkhurstbrothers.com**

Parkhurst Brothers books are distributed to the trade through the Chicago Distribution Center, and may be ordered through Ingram Book Company, Baker & Taylor, Follett Library Resources and other book industry wholesalers. To order from the University of Chicago's Chicago Distribution Center, phone 1-800-621-2736 or send a fax to 800-621-8476. Copies of this and other Parkhurst Brothers Inc., Publishers titles are available to organizations and corporations for purchase in quantity by contacting Special Sales Department at our home office location, listed on our web site.
This is a work of the author's imagination, a work of fiction.

Original Trade Paperback

Printed in the United States of America

First Edition, 2013

2012 2013 2014 2015 2016 2017 2018
15 14 13 12 11 10 9 8 7 6 5 4 3 2 1

Library of Congress Cataloging-in-Publication Data:

Hout, Judson N.
  Sweet hope : a novella / Judson N. Hout. ~ 1st ed.
    p. cm.
  ISBN-13: 978-1-935166-92-4
  ISBN-10: 1-935166-92-1
  ISBN-13: 978-1-935166-93-1
  ISBN-10: 1-935166-93-X
  1. Physicians~Fiction. 2. Arkansas~Fiction. I. Title.
  PS3608.O885S94 2013
  813'.6-dc23
                          2012013639

ISBN:  Trade Paperback:  978-1-935166-92-4   [10 digit: 1-935166-92-1]
ISBN:  e-book:  978-1-935166-93-1   [10-digit: 1-935166-93-X]

Design Director and Dustjacket/ cover design: Charlie Ross, North Little Rock, AR
Acquired for Parkhurst Brothers Inc. and edited by: Ted Parkhurst
Author photo by: Mary Brown

022013

*This book is dedicated to Carolyn, my wife, my love,*

*and to our blended family of six children, their spouses*

*and our sixteen grandchildren.*


*And in memory of Bradford Lusby,*

*a courageous young man who died too soon.*

# Acknowledgements

First and foremost, I owe many thanks to my wife, Carolyn, who encouraged me to write. I must admit that our love affair inspired me to write this story, though the *content* of the story is totally fiction.

I must thank Betty McCaffrey, who read an early rough draft of what was to become *Sweet Hope.* Without her encouragement, I likely never would have completed it.

I owe a debt of gratitude to Rex Nelson of Little Rock and Harry Thomason of Los Angeles who read my first book, the award winning *The Ghost of Bud Parrott*, and liked it. Their generous praise encouraged me to complete this novella.

Many, many thanks go to Melissa Gordon, who typed and re-typed the hand-written manuscript.

I am also indebted to Cindy Ward of Dallas for her endorsement of my first novel and her praise of the unfinished manuscript of this book.

Lynne Rowland of the Book and Frame Shop here in Camden has been most helpful to me in introducing me to a publisher she respected and recommending my work to him, an unexpected act of generosity for which I shall forever be indebted to her.

Many thanks go to Mary Catherine Jones of mcphotography for creating the photograph from which the cover of this book was made; and who, along with Wanda Gaston, produced the portrait of Carolyn and me, which appears on the back cover of this book.

I am greatly appreciative of the lovely Sarah Grace Murphree, the model for the girl on the cover.

Ted Parkhurst, the president of Parkhurst Brothers Publishers, has placed his financial resources and professional reputation on the line for me, for which I will forever be grateful.

*Judson N. Hout*
Camden, Arkansas
November 2012

"For of all sad words of tongue or pen
The saddest are these: 'It might have been.'"
**~John Greenleaf Whittier**


"Though nothing can bring back
The hour of splendor in the grass, glory in the flower,
We will grieve not, rather find strength
in what remains behind."
**~William Wordsworth**

Memory is strange. Memory of good times, running barefoot in cool spring grass, swimming with friends in a stream, first date, first kiss, and other pleasant events and happiness persists even into old age. Bad memories, unhappy memories tend to slowly go away, either by conscious effort or unconscious repression.

Not so for the memory of lost love. Unlike brief love affairs or mutually ended relationships, the memory of lost love persists forever. The sadness of it remains stored in some obscure cerebral vault to reappear at the most inappropriate moments. It pops up in dreams, during sleepless nights, and in familiar places or events shared with the lost loves. One wants to forget but cannot. Maybe in church, at the theater or on the beach the ghost of that love appears. So it was for Brad Duncan.

Each time the memory of Beth reappeared, it was always accompanied by the thought of what might have been. Many nights just as sleep neared he could see her in his mind's eye standing beside him at an altar repeating wedding vows. But then sleep would come, and only fitful dreams would appear.

He had been born and raised in Fabre's Bluff, a town of about ten thousand people in the pine forests of south Arkansas. The town stood on a bluff high above the Ouachita River and got its name from a Frenchman named Jacque Fabre, who many years ago had a trading post there. Young Brad and his friends often stood on the bluffs, imagining barges steaming upriver from New Orleans loaded with goods. In their minds eye they saw Indians and whites alike congregating here from area settlements to barter or purchase those goods. Sometimes, in their imaginations, they heard the crack of muskets as river pirates boarded and pillaged the barges. The spell broken, the friends ran off laughing in search of a pool in which to skinny-dip.

Brad's father, Jim Duncan, was a large robust man who owned and operated a sawmill that supplied lumber to south Arkansas, northern Louisiana and eastern Mississippi. Marian, Brad's mother, was a homemaker and part-time substitute teacher. Brad hated it when she taught his class.

His early life was filled with hunting and fishing with Big Jim in the woods, streams, and lakes of south Arkansas.

He first met Beth Collins when he was eleven years old. His family was on their annual vacation to Hardy, on the Spring River in north Arkansas. The river got its name because it arose full-size from a huge spring a few miles north in the town of Mammoth Spring. The river was very cold and had several rapids and a few small waterfalls no more than three feet high.

Wapton Inn, where they stayed, was atop a small hill overlooking the river. The place was reached first by crossing the river on a one-lane bridge, then traveling a winding, narrow gravel road to the top of a hill which seemed like a mountain to Brad. In reality, it was no more than sixty feet above the river at any point. A cool breeze rose from the icy-cold water through wild flowers and vines, emitting a fragrance unique to the area. There a large common area was encircled by screened cabins and a pavilion which served as a gathering place and the caretaker's office and residence. In the pavilion was a dance floor, food bar and a six-pin bowling alley. The pavilion was the gathering place for young and old alike. In the afternoons, when they weren't swimming or exploring, the young played ping-pong, bowled, or cajoled a kind of harmony from the lone pinball machine.

Behind the semi-circle of cabins was a foot path leading into a wooded area. The path, as it emerged from the woods, trailed slightly downward along the edge of a small cliff which seemed very high to the young boy. It was, however, no more than ten or fifteen feet high.

As the light faded into evening—and sometimes deep into the night—teenagers and young adults danced to the music of big bands on the Wurlitzer. To Brad, the place was magic.

As he always did the first day there, Brad explored the woods along the path and then along the edge of the cliff. He was sitting on a large rock when he first saw her.

He heard a rustle of leaves and looked up the path and there she was. As she walked toward him down the path, she was backlit by the late afternoon sun so that she appeared to be a shadow inside a large halo of sunlight. He was very taken aback by the image of her.

As she approached him, stepping out of the light, he saw her all dressed in starched white shirt, shorts, socks and tennis shoes. She was lovely and quite angelic in appearance. Her brown hair was pulled back into a ponytail; and her eyes were large and brown, so brown that her pupils appeared to be part of the irises. Her figure was trim, and her smile was enchanting.

"Hi," she said, "I'm Beth. I'm eleven, well almost eleven. I will be in September. Who are you?"

For a moment he was speechless, but then he said, "I'm Brad."

"Well, Brad, how old are you?"

"I'm already eleven," he replied.

"I have this thing about names," she said. "What's your whole name?"

"Brad Duncan."

"Is it Brad or Bradley, and do you have a middle name?"

"It's Bradley Andrew Duncan," he said, becoming a little irritated.

"Your initials spell bad. Are you bad?"

"No," he replied, a little too forcefully.

"I'll bet your friends tease you by saying, 'Bradley, Bradley smells very badly', don't they?"

He felt himself getting angry when he replied, "No, they do not!"

"Oh, Brad, don't let me get your goat. Don't you know I'm only teasing, and people only tease people they like. I can tell I'm going to like you a lot".

She had him then. He was enthralled by her. She was just beautiful and unlike any girl he had ever known before.

"What's your whole name? Do your initials spell anything?", was all he could think to say.

"I don't have a middle name. It's just plain Beth Collins, maybe BC like Before Christ or something. When I'm grown and on my own, I'm going to hire a lawyer and have it changed to Elizabeth Anne, with an e, Collins. It still won't spell anything, but at least it will be dignified."

"I like Beth," was all he could say.

They talked for a bit, and after awhile she started to leave. As she walked away she turned and said, "Well Brad, what are we going to do tomorrow?"

"How about running the rapids in my Dad's boat?", he replied.

"Oh, that sounds like fun. Let's do it."

"Okay," he said, "meet me at the dock at about nine. Bring your bathing suit."

"I'll be there," and she began walking up the path.

As she walked up the path she again cast a shadow in the setting sun. The sun was lower on the horizon now, which made the halo larger and brighter. Her shadow was lighter at first so he could see her look back at him. He could barely make out her smile but could easily see her wave. Then she became darker and smaller, and finally disappeared into what became a large, intense globe of light. For the first and last time in his life he was in love, only he didn't know it at the time.

Sleep did not come easy for him that night. What sleep he got was fitful, and each time he awoke and looked at the bedside clock he was disappointed that it wasn't yet time to get up. Finally he fell into such a deep sleep that he had to be awakened by his mother for breakfast.

He was alarmed when he saw it was already 8:45. He hurried to the bathroom, brushed his teeth and combed his hair. He dressed quickly, putting on his bathing suit under his jeans.

As he rushed to the door, Marian said, "Wait just a minute, young man. You are not going to leave without having breakfast."

He hurriedly scoffed down a piece of toast and a glass of milk and rushed out carrying a grocery list his mother had given him.

Beth was waiting when he arrived at the dock. "You're late," she said. "I believe in being on time. Another minute and I would have left".

"I overslept," was all he could say.

"I would think you wouldn't have been able to sleep at all after meeting me," she said with a laugh.

He had no idea what to say. Never had he been teased so much by anyone, much less a girl. And why was he so bothered by her, he thought. He didn't even like girls, but yet he couldn't keep his eyes off her.

Finally he said, "Come on, let's get in the boat. My mom gave me a list of groceries to get in town. She said I could go by boat. There's a life preserver for you under the middle seat. Did you bring your bathing suit?"

"I have it on under my clothes. You didn't think I would change behind a bush with you sneaking a peek, did you?"

Again he was speechless. Not wanting to look stupid, he just smiled and said nothing.

"Where is your life preserver?" she asked.

"I don't need one."

"Well if you don't wear one, neither will I."

So he put on a life jacket, and she put on hers. Beth took the middle seat, and he sat in the back and jerked on the rope until the ten-horse motor started. For an instant, admiring her soft shoulders from behind, he regretted insisting she wear the life preserver. Only a moment later, however, motoring downstream at top speed, he yelled, "Hold on. We're about to go over the falls." As the boat jumped the small waterfall spraying both of them—Beth the most—the wisdom of wearing life vests was confirmed.

"Watch it boy," she shouted. "I don't want to get drenched."

He laughed and said, "Watch this," and he moved to the front of the boat and guided the boat by shifting his weight from side to side. He was disappointed when Beth showed no sign of fear or alarm. She just accused him of being a show-off.

As they neared the town he moved to the back of the boat and steered it to the bank, beached it, and tied it to a tree.

"Come on," he said, and they walked the fifty yards to the grocery store. He gave the owner the list, and the order was filled promptly.

As he paid, the owner said, "Aren't you going to buy your girlfriend some candy?"

"She's not my girlfriend," he said, "she's just a friend."

"Don't let him fool you, mister. I am his girlfriend. He's already thinking about marrying me when we grow up".

Both Beth and the grocer had a good laugh, but Brad just stood there, his cheeks, neck and ears blushing, especially his ears, which felt as if they were about to burn off. She was right, though. He had thought about marrying her some day.

After he took the groceries to the cabin, they spent the rest of the morning swimming, riding the rapids in inner tubes and jumping the falls in the boat.

By noon the ice-cold river water had turned their lips blue and their fingertips wrinkled. They were shivering. Having enough of the cold water, they dressed and went to the pavilion for hot dogs. The rest of the afternoon was spent bowling, playing ping-pong, and just visiting.

About four o'clock Beth said, "Bradley dear, why don't you put a nickel in the juke box and let's dance."

"I don't dance," he said, not wanting to be teased by other kids in the pavilion.

"But Bradley, if you don't dance with me, you sure can't kiss me!"

"Who said anything about kissing?" was all he could say. "But what are we gonna do tomorrow?"

"Whatever you want, Brad. I know I tease a lot, but I'm not kidding now. I really had a nice time today. Come by my cabin about nine tomorrow, and I'll introduce you to my mom and dad."

He was tired, yet almost giddy when he opened the screen door of his cabin. "Hey, Mom, what's up!?" he asked almost too cheerfully.

His mother laughed and said, "Well, young man, it looks like you had a fun day with that pretty little girl."

Embarrassed, he lowered his voice and said, "It was okay."

"Yes, I can see it was," Marian said with a grin.

He slept soundly that night and awoke before the alarm clock sounded. After brushing his teeth, showering, and making sure his hair was combed just right, he splashed on a little of his father's cologne and went in for breakfast.

Finally it was nine o'clock, and he skipped to Beth's cabin. Through locked screened doors and windows, he saw stripped beds, swept fireplace, no sign of occupants. The cabin was empty. Brad ran to the caretaker's cabin, breathlessly asking where the Collins family was.

"They left before daylight, son," was all the caretaker could tell him.

"Where did they go? Did they leave for good?"

"For good. They paid their bill and left," he replied.

Brad felt his head drop forward. His arms weighed a hundred pounds each.

"Did the little girl leave me a note?"

"No, son, I'm afraid she didn't."

"Please, mister, I don't even know where they live. Will you give me their address so I can write to her?" he pleaded.

"I'm sorry, son, but I'm not allowed to give out that information."

Nausea rose in his chest. His belly cramped. Brad thought he might vomit or worse, have diarrhea in his pants. He was able to avoid both urges, but not heartbreak so loud it crowded out the caretaker's voice and every other noise of the camp. When tears began to form in his eyes, Brad told himself he was too old for that. Only by focusing on the mantra You're too old for that with fierce determination did he avoid embarrassing himself.

Slowly Brad turned and ambled unsteadily down the path to the place where he had first seen her. He had no idea if he would ever see her again.

The rest of the week was difficult for Brad. He missed Beth terribly. He missed the smell of her and even how she teased him. Why did they leave; where did they go? kept rushing through his brain like the rapids on the river. How would he ever find her, and why did he care so much? He had never even held a girl's hand before, much less kissed one. Something had to be wrong with him!

Getting to sleep at night and waking up in the morning became trouble for him. Usually he was late for breakfast.

Finally his mother asked, "Honey, what's wrong with you? Do you have a headache or something?"

"I'm okay," was all he could say, but he could tell she knew better.

"Well, eat up. I have a grocery list for you. You can take the boat because Dad went fishing with a friend in the friend's boat. Ours is available. Maybe time on the river will help you feel better."

He ate, although he was not hungry. When he got to the dock, several kids were hanging around, but he just said hello and went on his way.

Well into the boat ride, Brad noticed that he was whistling a tune his father sometimes whistled or hummed. On the river, the air was cool enough to give him goose bumps on the backs of his hands, and the cold spray of the water as he rode the rapids and jumped the waterfalls felt good on his neck and ears. However, his mood again became dour when the grocer asked where his girlfriend was.

All he could say was, "She left;" the grocer scratched behind his ear, saying no more. Brad guessed it was obvious to him that he missed her.

When he got back to camp and was approaching the cabin, he overheard his parents talking. He stopped to eavesdrop.

"Jim, I'm glad you're back. I'm worried about Brad. Something isn't right with him, but he won't open up to me. You need to talk to him."

"Oh hell, Mim," Jim said. "He's just got the candy-leg for that little Collins girl. Give him a little time, and he'll get over it. I do wonder why the Collins left so suddenly though. Joe and I were walking down to the dock before daylight and saw them leaving. They woke the caretaker up to check out. Something must have happened to one of them."

Brad walked in and said, "I don't care about that girl. She was just somebody to mess around with."

His dad just tousled his hair and said, "Come on, boy, let's run up the river a way, and I'll show you how to catch some trout."

He loved being with his dad who could be funny as well as serious. He liked fishing with him and just having quiet conversations with him. They had fun that day, caught lots of fish, and talked about many things. But Brad could not talk to him about Beth.

Finally Jim said, "Brad, I know what's bothering you. You fell for that little Collins girl. She was a pretty thing, and I don't blame you. I know how it hurts, because I had two or three sweethearts before I met your mom. Some I lost, and some lost me. Boy, you'll have a bunch of girlfriends before you're grown and find the right one. I promise you, you'll get over this one."

"I know," was all Brad could say, although he didn't believe it. He had made up his mind; Beth was the one. Somehow, some way, some day he would find her.


The rest of the summer was relatively quiet in Fabre's Bluff. Saturdays were spent fishing with his dad on the Ouachita or on small river lakes. With Jim's help, he became a fairly good bass fisherman. Sundays were for church and just quiet afternoons wandering through the town and the surrounding woods.

The rest of the week was spent doing chores, running errands for his mother or playing with his friends- a fairly bucolic existence. All the rest of the summer, in spite of what he was doing, Beth almost daily crept into his mind. He daydreamed about her, and in his mind's eye, could see them as adults walking down the aisle of the Episcopal Church to be married. Those mental images did nothing to improve his mood.

School starting in the fall did help though. He enjoyed school and all the extracurricular activities, particularly the football games.

Being a sixth grader, he was at the top echelon of the elementary school. He began to notice girls, none of whom could stir up his emotion the way Beth did. Invariably whenever he noticed how pretty and nice certain girls were, the image of Beth popped into his head.

The sixth grade term went by fast, and the next summer the Duncans went back to Hardy, this time for two weeks. It wasn't the same, though, with Beth not there. He had so hoped that she and her family would be there, but they were nowhere around. Brad wanted to ask the caretaker about Beth and her family, but he did not want to appear anxious. He wanted to be nonchalant. He hung around the pavilion most of that first day hoping for an opportunity to ask about them without giving away the depth of his need. First, he bowled alone. Then he wandered to the pinball machine and played two short games there. From there, he walked aimlessly about the grounds which seemed larger than before, and empty.

After what seemed like an eternity, Brad approached a group of boys about his age who invited him to join them for a swim in the river. The water seemed shockingly colder than last year, so the swim was quickly abandoned. Brad kicked a pine cone through the dirt all the way back to his family cabin.

The second day there Brad got up the courage to approach the caretaker. "Sir", he said, "do you remember the Collins family that was here last summer? Are they coming back this year?"

"You mean the family with the pretty little girl you were sweet on?"

Brad blushed as he replied, "I wasn't sweet on her, but I liked her a lot. We had a lot of fun doing things together."

"No", said the caretaker, "we have heard no more from them since last summer."

So the rest of the vacation he just wandered around, fished with his dad, ran errands for his mother, and played with the other kids. It wasn't the same without Beth there, so he was glad when the two weeks were up. The only reason he would ever want to come back was in the hope of finding Beth.

The seventh and eighth grades passed quickly and uneventfully except for the fact that in the spring of the eighth grade year puberty struck with a vengeance. He experienced a rapid growth spurt and an embarrassing voice change.

The following summer his life changed drastically. Jim Duncan began to have pains in his abdomen that rapidly became severe and incapacitating. After a few weeks he was diagnosed with pancreatic cancer. The prognosis was grim.

Getting his affairs in order, Jim sold the sawmill for much less than it was worth because he was underinsured, and he knew that Marian and Brad would need the money. Marian sensed how hard it was going to be. The savings would soon evaporate. She tried to shield Brad from her worry, but he was a prescient boy. Worse than any monetary concern was the foreboding of life without his father. Brad began almost immediately to feel how terribly he would miss his father.

The pain became unbearable, and the heavy doses of narcotics almost completely obliterated Jim's personality. In the end, he was emaciated, his weight down to eighty pounds. In June after Brad's eighth grade year, his father died.

Brad was devastated by Jim's death. How could he die? Brad thought. He was only forty years old. He never smoked; he never drank. All he did was hunt and fish and work. Brad prayed at least three times a day, yet his father weakened almost visibly. Brad was willing to barter with God, but watching the disease was a daily defeat. Like watching the sun go down after a forest fire, Brad thought. It was too late for anything he could imagine. When the inevitable happened, Brad was mad at God for taking his father from him. At the funeral, all Brad could think was God is a cheat.

That summer Marian had to go to work. She got a job as the school counselor and as such she was supplied a car, because the job required her to travel from school to school. She taught Brad to drive the family car, a three year old Chevrolet, and kept Jim's pickup to use herself for the family's personal needs.

Going into the ninth grade, Brad had grown to six feet two inches on a skinny frame. His voice had stabilized into a moderate bass, and his feet had grown to a size twelve. Due to his big feet, he was given the nickname "Feets" by his friends. He was embarrassed by it but gave it no particular care, because he had lost his father, and he had lost Beth.

By the beginning of school in the tenth grade, the gloom he and his mother had lived with had all but gone. He had grown to six-four and 180 pounds, and his feet had remained at size twelve. An uncle said that his body had finally caught up with his feet.

He became a fairly good football player and a very good basketball player. He also made good grades in school so that by his senior year he was near the top of his class scholastically.

Throughout his high school career, whenever they played a basketball game out of town, he always looked through the crowd in the stands hoping to see Beth. Always during warm-up and sometimes during breaks in the game, he would look through the old wooden bleachers to see her face. Once he thought he did see her. A girl's laugh reminded him of Beth, but he quickly realized her eyes were wrong. The girl saw him staring and winked at him, then turned to her friends and laughed again. Brad felt foolish, even disloyal to Beth. He never did find her.

His grades and good SAT score guaranteed him scholarship money for college. He had hoped for a basketball scholarship offer from the University of Arkansas, but that never came through, although he did have offers from small colleges.

Because of his father's illness and death, Brad had decided to study to be a doctor. He knew that his chances of getting admitted to medical school would be better if he attended the University, so he gave up the idea of playing college basketball. He applied for admission to the University of Arkansas in Fayetteville and was accepted. He had no idea how his life was about to change.

Brad's last summer at home in Fabre's Bluff was difficult because he hated to leave his mother to live alone. She had been very strong for him, and he loved her dearly. She was always in good cheer and encouraged him to look forward instead of backward.

The summer was almost unbearably hot and dry. To make money for college, Brad got a job in an asphalt plant. His initial job was shoveling sand and gravel out of railroad gondola cars. The work was hard but invigorating.

Within a couple of weeks he was moved to the weight station, a very easy but hot job. He sat in a shack and weighed each dump truck coming into the plant empty. Then he weighed the truck going out loaded. From the difference in the two weights Brad calculated the charge to the road builder for the asphalt. There was a continuous line of trucks, in and out, for ten to twelve hours a day, six and sometimes seven days a week.

By the end of summer he had saved almost two thousand dollars, which with academic scholarships and campus jobs, would get him through his first year of school fine.

Finally September came. It was time to leave for Fayetteville. Marian was able to give him the Chevrolet, because she had the school car and the pickup. He wanted her to have the car and him to have the pickup, but she refused. She said she hated for him to take girls on dates in an old beat up truck.

As they were packing the car, Marian said, "Honey, I don't want you to worry about me. I have my friends, my work, and my church. I'll be fine."

"I know, Mom," he replied, "but I hate for you to be alone. At least I've been here to aggravate you some." They both laughed.

"Boy, get your fanny in that car and get going. Have fun, study hard, and before you know it you will be a rich doctor and able to support me in my old age. I envy you, though, because you are about to go on a great adventure. You are now a man and a very good man at that. I am so very proud of you, and your Daddy would be proud of you too. You were his pride and joy."

So he was on his way – an eighteen year old man on a quest to become a small town doctor.

The three hundred mile trip to Fayetteville took Brad almost seven hours. By the time he stopped in front of Gregson Hall, where all male rushees were to stay, he was very hot and tired.

He had been encouraged by friends who were members of Kappa Sigma to go through rush. They told him to not appear to be anxious but to just play it cool, so he didn't look any of them up. He moved into Gregson and waited for invitations to attend rush parties at various fraternity houses. Several invitations came, and he attended all to which he was invited.

Raucous and downright bawdy skits were put on at all the houses. The skit at the Kappa Sigma house was no different from the rest. On a makeshift stage, a tall, thin boy, barefoot and dressed in overalls and a straw hat was standing facing a tall urinal. Next to him, a short boy with hair parted in the middle stood in another urinal, which he called a midget shower. The two spoke in hayseed accents about conquests of country girls and farm animals, punctuating their stilted dialogue with loud farts. The audience clearly enjoyed laughing at the pathetic performance, especially when the short boy was doused at the end of the act. After the skit, Brad and a few others were taken into the house mother's quarters. She had an electric organ which she played for them while they sang. As they left the quarters, one of the brothers said, "All house mothers have organs, but ours has a Hammond electric organ." That brought laughs from all within earshot.

At the end of the week Brad chose Kappa Sigma, was accepted by them, and moved into the fraternity house.

One of the requirements of all the pledges was to have at least one date a week. If a pledge could not secure a date by himself, his sponsor, or big brother, as he was called, would get one for him.

Brad knew no girls; so Joe Henderson, his big brother, got him a date with Marie Lepanto, a Pi Phi from Lake Village, for the first football game and the dance following the game. Marie was of Italian descent and was attractive, though no beauty. Between the game and the dance, they had dinner at an Italian restaurant.

"So where is Fabre's Bluff?" Marie asked.

"It's about a hundred miles south of Little Rock on the Ouachita

River," Brad replied.

"I never heard of it," said Marie. "That's a strange name for a town- Fabre's Bluff. How did it get that name?"

"I'm not sure, but I was told a Frenchman named Fabre had a trading post on a high bluff overlooking the river back when Arkansas was just a territory. A settlement developed and grew into a town, so they named the town Fabre's Bluff."

"I'm from Lake Village on Lake Chicot near the Mississippi River so I guess we are sort of neighbors. I guess we're both river rats," Marie said.

"I know Lake Village," said Brad, "and Lake Chicot too. My dad and I fished for crappie there one time. We caught a bunch. Crappie is my favorite fish to eat. Dad told me a lot of Italian people settled there."

"That's true," she said. "I am fourth generation Italian. My great grandfather brought his family to this country from Italy. I'm not sure where in Italy. They didn't like New Orleans – too many French, my dad said. My great grandfather came by boat up the Mississippi and settled in Lake Village. There were already many Italians living there."

Brad just nodded.

"I know about fishing, though," Marie continued. "Both my brothers fished all the time. They always smelled like fish. I didn't like fishing – too hot and too many mosquitoes. Like most Italians I love to party, and we're at the right school for parties. I hear they even pipe beer into all the rooms at the Kappa Sig house."

At the dance that night, Marie became quite uninhibited due to too many beers. While dancing, she made sure her breasts brushed against Brad's chest and her leg went too far between his thighs. Brad had never been a drinker, but to not seem a prude he drank several beers and became somewhat lightheaded. His speech became slightly slurred, and he staggered while dancing. Leaving the dance floor, Brad stumbled and fell into a table occupied by two couples. The boys helped him to his feet and assisted him to his table where he sat until his head cleared. He vowed that after he sobered up he would never drink that much again.

At the Pi Phi door at midnight date call, Marie threw her left arm around Brad's neck and gave him a passionate kiss. At the same time with her right hand she roughly rubbed his crotch.

A couple of weeks later all the pledges who had not had a date that week were required to get a date for church and then Sunday dinner at the fraternity house. Knowing no one else, Brad asked Marie. They went to mass at the Episcopal Church, although Marie was Catholic. The Episcopal Church was a compromise.

At dinner between the main course and dessert, the initiates sang fraternity songs. Brad was embarrassed when they sang, "Get your hands above the table, Brad Duncan. Keep your hands above the table, Brad Duncan. We've seen you do it twice, and it isn't very nice. Keep your hands above the table, Brad Duncan." Marie just laughed.

Finally the semester ended, and Brad had a four point. He was initiated in January.

He hadn't really been interested in dating but had kept up his pledge duties by dating Marie. At the post-initiation party, he and Marie had danced and generally had a good time.

Near midnight at the Pi Phi door, Marie said, "Brad, we've had a lot of dates and a lot of fun, but in all that time you've never made a move on me. Why?"

"I don't know," he said. "Maybe there's something wrong with me. I just don't feel like it. You are a beautiful girl, and I like you a lot but not in that way, I guess."

"Well, screw you buddy," and she sashayed through the door and slammed it behind her.

The rest of the spring semester was uneventful. Brad had no dates. Being a full-fledged member, he was allowed to work in the dining room serving meals, busing tables and washing dishes. It took a few days for him to quiet the gag reflex that accompanied pungent, rancid grease and garbage. After his first week, the nausea was forgotten. His compensation was free room and board. Next, Brad got a second job picking up and delivering clothes in the house for a local laundry and cleaners, securing a modest budget of spending money.

He liked the kitchen job except for the days when beef tongue was served. The tongues were cut in long slices and looked just like what they were. One of the other kitchen-working brothers always brought his platter of tongues into the dining room with a slice of tongue hanging out his mouth. Brad thought that was disgusting.

In biology class Brad met a girl named Angela Tucker, who was a sophomore pre-nursing student and almost a year older than he. They had a few dates but nothing significant developed. She had one more year in Fayetteville and then would transfer to the University Medical Center in Little Rock to attend nursing school. She wanted to get a Bachelor of Nursing as well as her RN degree.

Brad found Angela to be very pleasant company but somewhat reserved. That suited him fine, because he wasn't interested in a serious relationship.

Finally the semester ended, and Brad headed back to Fabre's Bluff and his summer job at the asphalt plant.

Fabre's Bluff looked the same, yet it wasn't the same. During the year he'd been away, a new shopping center had opened at the edge of town. Several merchants had abandoned the courthouse square, leaving handmade signs in their empty windows. Several storefronts were even boarded up. The Malco Theater was closed, the moveable letters on its marquee now rearranged by high school kids whose vocabulary grew increasingly crude. The Rialto, where community theater products had been held for years, was now just a shell with a collapsed roof. Brad was sad to see his old haunts in such a condition. He was nineteen and had spent nearly a year away in a vibrant society, and this place, though home, was very different from Fayetteville and campus life. Time crept, and no one was in a hurry.

His job was unchanged- long hot days in a shack with no fans. The pay was good; and with his job at the fraternity house, he would not need money from his mother for the next school year. He had been offered an easier and better paying job at the sawmill, but he couldn't face that which had been so important to his dead father.

At dinner one evening, Marian said, "Honey, you have no social life here. What about at school? Did you date anyone? You rarely wrote, and when you did, you never talked about anything but studies and the fraternity."

"Oh, I dated a couple of girls but nothing serious," he replied.

He must have come across as sad or preoccupied because she said, "Brad, I've known you since the instant you were born, and I've loved you longer than that. Something is not right with you. I can tell. I'm not going to pressure you, but I am worried. I just want you to know that I'm ready to listen at any time you want to talk."

"I know, Mom," Brad replied. "I don't know what's wrong with me. School was good. My grades were great. Nothing has bothered me, but I just don't feel right. I'm happy. I like school and frat life. Something is just missing."

"What about the girls?"

"It's nothing like that. One of the girls, her name was Marie, wanted to get serious. She was nice and very attractive and fun to be around, but I just couldn't get with it. In the end she just slammed the door in my face, and that was the end of it. There must be something wrong with me."

"Nonsense," she said. "There isn't a thing wrong with you. What about the other girl?"

"Angela? She's okay. Very pretty and very quiet. She's in pre-nursing and will be going to the Med Center in another year. I think she could get serious about me, but I don't feel that way about her."

They were quiet for a while, and then Brad just had to say it. "Mom, do you remember the summer when I was eleven, and we spent a week in Hardy?"

"Of course I do. That was when your daddy said you were stuck on that pretty little girl. What was her name?"

"Beth Collins. Mom, I have never been able to get her out of my head. Ever since then I've looked for her everywhere – in the stands at basketball games, around the campus. I don't know where she lives or even if she's dead or alive."

" So that's what's been eating at you all this time," she exclaimed.

"It has. Even on dates with other girls I think of her. I wonder how my life would have been if she were around."

"Honey, have you heard the phrase, "For of all sad words of

tongue or pen, the saddest are these, it might have been'?"

"Yes ma'am, I have."

"Do you know where it came from?"

"No ma'am," he replied.

"It came from the poem, Maud Muller, by John Greenleaf Whittier. It's about a young couple, he was rich and she was poor, who had a brief encounter and then went their separate ways, but neither was able to forget the other. In the last verse, Maud said just what you said – it might have been. Then the poet wrote the lines about all sad words. But right after those words he wrote, 'Ah well, for us all some sweet hope lies deeply buried from human eyes'. Who knows, maybe somewhere when you least expect it she may appear. That may be your sweet hope."

Brad felt better for finally talking to someone about Beth. He remembered long ago telling himself that someday he would find her. He decided to keep hoping.

Finally summer ended, and Brad was on his way back to Fayetteville.

He wanted to live in an apartment with a friend to be away from the noise and confusion of the fraternity house, but needing the jobs, he had to remain in the house. He was lucky, though, because an upper classman had been assigned a two-man room on the third floor and had asked Brad to room with him. It would be quiet and comfortable. At the end of a narrow hall, it was a room with four irregular walls, a window in the smallest. Below the window was a desk with two small chairs. On the wall opposite the desk stood bunk beds. Brad got the top bunk. The view from the only window was into a large oak tree which hid Dickson Street below. Brad realized that during the winter, after the leaves had fallen, he would have a good view of the expansive university commons across the street.

Joe Bill was a senior pre-med student and was very studious. He was not a party type. That suited Brad fine. His sophomore year would be better, he thought, in a quiet room with a serious roommate.

There were plenty of parties, some Brad went to and some he didn't. Rush week was the same, and the Kappa Sigs got all the pledges they wanted.

During the first month of school, he ran into Marie at the Student Union. After exchanging pleasantries, Marie said, "Brad, I'm sorry about what happened last year. I'm dating a Sigma Chi now. I hope you and I can be friends."

"Of course we can, Marie," Brad replied. "You're looking good. How are things at the Pi Phi house?"

"Just fine. We got a really good group of pledges. You ought to come over and meet some of them."

"Maybe I will," he said without much enthusiasm.

The next day Brad was walking to class when he saw Marie and another girl walking toward him. He couldn't believe his eyes!

"Beth!" he exclaimed, "I can't believe it's you."

"Hi Brad," she said. "You've gotten tall and still have big feet."

"You two know each other?" Marie asked.

Brad could say nothing but just looked at her. She was even more beautiful than he remembered, tall and full-figured, with the deepest brown eyes he had ever seen.

Finally he said, "We met when I was eleven, and she was almost eleven. What happened to you all, Beth? Why did you leave so suddenly?"

Marie was speechless but seemed a little put out.

"Why don't we meet at the Union about three, and I'll tell you about it," said Beth.

"I'll be there," he said, knowing he would have to cut a class to do so.

Brad got to the Union fifteen minutes early and found a table in a corner spot secluded by a waist-high wall and a large fake plant. At precisely three, Beth stepped in and scanned the room, looking for him. He stood and waved, and she returned his wave with a smile of her own. He was glad she was alone.

She sat down beside him and said, "Did you have something going with Marie? She sure is acting strange, almost sullen."

"We dated a few times last year. She wanted to get serious, but I didn't. It ended sort of badly. But tell me what happened back then."

"Oh Brad, it was terrible. Daddy woke up about three with chest pain. He thought it was indigestion. The night before he had eaten too much, smoked too much, and drunk too much. Mother wanted to take him to a hospital in Hardy, but he refused to go."

She was quiet for a moment. Brad said nothing.

She continued, "He insisted on going home to Paragould, a good two hour drive. He would have it no other way, so Mother packed and loaded the car and checked out. Daddy stretched out in the back seat, and I rode in the front with Mother. We left about five that morning and pulled up at the Paragould hospital about seven. When the attendants came to get him out of the car he was dead."

"That's terrible," was all Brad could say.

"Mother and I made it okay. There was a lot of life insurance. Daddy was only thirty five, but he was overweight and a heavy smoker. His heart just played out."

"Beth, I am so sorry. I've thought about you all these years. Everywhere I went I looked for you, hoping to find you. I guess we just lived in the farthest corners of the state."

"That's not all. Mother died of ovarian cancer when I was in the ninth grade. I had to go live with my grandparents in Fulton, Missouri."

"My father died of pancreatic cancer, so I know how you feel."

"I wanted to stay close to Mamaw and Papaw, so I went to William Woods College in Fulton last year. I wasn't happy there, and my grandparents insisted I transfer here. This was always my first choice. I admit I was hoping to find you here."

So his mother was right when she said somewhere when he least expected it she would appear. He still loved her. He knew it now. He just couldn't tell her yet.

"Beth," he said, "Will you mark my name down on all the dates on your social calendar for the next year?"

"Why, Brad, I thought you'd never ask."

She still had her sense of humor.

For the rest of the school year, Brad dated only Beth. Every athletic event, every social event, it was Beth and Brad. Most Sunday evenings they had their evening meal at the Venetian Inn in Tontitown, most often alone but sometimes with another couple.

One Sunday night in a movie theater as they were holding hands Beth squeezed his hand three times. After the movie she asked him if he noticed the squeeze. He admitted he did.

She asked, "Do you know the three most repeated words in the English language?"

"No," he replied.

"Of course you do, just think. The three most spoken words in the English language, or any language for that matter, are I love you. That is what I'm saying with three squeezes – those three words. When I can't say it out loud, I'll say it with three squeezes of your hand."

So she had beaten him to it. She had said it first. From then on, that would be their silent code.

"Beth," he said, "I guess I am bashful or shy or something or just plain stupid. I have been in love with you since I first saw you, walking down that path in Hardy. I promise I will love you forever."

And then they kissed right there on the courthouse square, oblivious of the crowd leaving the movie theater. Her lips were soft and moist. It was not a provocative kiss, but rather a gentle loving kiss, and it made a chill go through his entire body. The touch of her hand at the back of his neck made his skin tingle. The feel of her body pressed tightly against his caused such a rush of affection for her that he actually feared he would cry. As they parted, they heard an elderly woman say, "Well, I never!" Their eyes met and they both laughed, walking hand-in-hand down the street to a small café.

One night after a dance at the Uark Bowl, they were parked in the pea patch – a sort of lovers' lane. After a while passion got the better of Brad, and he made a move on her.

Beth pulled back and said, "Brad, stop and let's talk for a minute."

The tone of her voice was forceful yet kind. He stopped.

She said, "There is nothing wrong with me. I want to just as much as you do, maybe more; but I am not going to go that far. I have never had sex, and I hope you realize that I have never asked you if you have. If you have, I don't want to know – that is your business. Whatever you have done in the past is of no concern to me, only what you do in the future. I think sex is wonderful and the purest way to share love, but I only want to share it with one person my entire life. That will have to be the only man I have ever loved, and that man is you. But we are not married. When we are married, that will come naturally and purely. I hope you can respect my wishes."

What could he say? It was not what he wanted, but he loved her enough to accept it.

"Beth, I love you enough, more than I ever thought I could love anyone. I have never had sex, that's the truth. I will respect you and love you until I die. But when we are married ---." And they both laughed.


The rest of the school year went by fast, and they remained true to their resolve about no sex until marriage.

Brad decided to stay in Fayetteville for the summer to get organic chemistry out of the way. He got a job at Wal-Mart to support himself. The fraternity house was closed for the summer, so he rented a small two room apartment.

Beth felt she should spend at least most of the summer to be with her aging grandparents.

One night, about a week into summer school, there was a knock at his door. Brad opened it to find Abigail Winningham, a girl from Fabre's Bluff, standing there. Her face was puffy and her eyes were red from crying. Her nose was running from so many tears. She wiped it on her sleeve. Her hair was uncombed and it looked to Brad as if she had slept in her dress. She was a distant relative, a second or third cousin. He asked her in and, taking her hand, led her to the couch. She sat at the edge of the seat with her hands in her lap, twisting a tissue.

When she began to speak, her voice broke into sobs. Finally she said, "Brad, I don't know who to turn to for help. I'm in trouble. I don't know what to do."

"Abi, you're not pregnant!"

"Yes I am. Almost seven months. Oh, Brad, what can I do? Mother will just die, and Daddy will kill me. You know how he is."

"Abigail, give me a day or two to think about it. I'll come up with something. I didn't even know you were in school here."

"I'm not," she said. "I flunked out. I'm working as a secretary in a lawyer's office."

During the next three days he saw her several times. During that time he made contact with the Florence Crittenton Home for Unwed Mothers in Little Rock and made arrangements for Abigail to stay there for the last few weeks of her pregnancy. The home would arrange for her care, her delivery and the adoption of the child. There would be no cost to Abigail. She would give Brad's address to her parents as hers, and he would forward their mail to her.

Her boss was understanding and agreed to let her take a leave of absence. She would be at the home such a short time that they felt they could pull it off.

The first of July Brad took Abigail to the bus. The bus door was open and the engine running. The thick diesel exhaust made Brad's eyes water and he coughed. Abigail stood on her tiptoes and kissed Brad on the cheek. He hugged her, kissed on the cheek, and led her to the door. He was very relieved to see her leave.

The next afternoon Marie Lepanto was at Brad's door with a note from Beth. It read:

*Brad,*
*I see you have not kept your promise. I'll not be coming*
*back to Fayetteville. I hope you and your pregnant girlfriend*
*will be happy.*
*Beth*

"Marie," he almost shouted, "That girl is my cousin. I didn't even know she was in Fayetteville. I was just helping her out of a bad situation."

"Well, Beth came to Fayetteville to surprise you and saw you kiss the girl at the bus station. She gave me the note and left."

"Do you know where she went? I've got to find her and explain."

"Yes, I know," she said, "but I promised never to tell you. She is transferring to another school in another state."

"Do you know how to get in touch with her?"

"I'll tell you what. Write her a letter, and I'll mail it to her. She has your phone number and your address. She can contact you. That way I can help you without betraying her."

Brad wrote the letter explaining the whole thing. He told her he loved her and always would. He begged her to understand and come back or at least tell him where she was so he could come to her.

Marie took the letter and left. All Brad could do was wait.

A few days later, Marie came to his apartment. She said, "Brad, I'm sorry, but Beth phoned me and asked me to tell you she doesn't believe you. She said it's over and asked that you never try to find her."

So that was that. Brad had lost her for the second time and this time with no hope of finding her. He was despondent and needed time to think. He found himself wandering the campus aimlessly, eventually approaching the cemetery behind the Kappa Sig house. The walk had calmed him some and the cemetery was quiet. While sitting at the base of a large tree, he finally came to a conclusion. What could he do but finish summer school, get through his junior year of college, and hopefully get accepted to medical school? He knew, however, that his life would never be the same.

Brad was inconsolable. He wanted to be around no one. He just went to organic class, to work, and home to the little apartment. His mind was pummeled with thoughts of Beth. What could he do? He didn't know where she lived nor did he even know the names of her grandparents. He went to Fulton and phoned everyone in the phone book named Collins, but no one knew her. He realized her grandparents must have been her mother's parents, and he didn't know her mother's maiden name.

Eventually he just gave up after again begging information from Marie without success.

However, he had changed. He got through the summer and went to Fabre's Bluff for a weekend prior to the beginning of the fall semester. Marian noticed the change. "Brad, what is the matter with you? What's wrong?" she asked.

"Mom, I've lost Beth and this time for good. It's a long story. Abigail came to me seven months pregnant wanting help. I arranged for her to go to Florence Crittenton's to have the baby. Beth had been in Fulton. She came back in time to see me put Abi on the bus for Little Rock.

"Beth thought Abi was a girl I had gotten pregnant and left. She left me a note telling me goodbye. I don't know where she went or how to find her. Marie, a mutual friend, is the only one who knows where she is, but she won't tell me. She did agree to mail a letter to her for me, but Beth phoned her and told her she didn't believe me and to tell me to leave her alone forever."

"My God," was all Marian could say. She took him in her arms and hugged him until her arms ached. He hugged her back and sobbed softly. His pain caused her to cry, as well.

"I don't know what to do, Mom. I love her with all my heart. I don't think I can live without her."

"Brad, honey, you've got to. Life goes on. I thought I couldn't live without your daddy, but I did. You've got your whole life ahead of you. You've got too much that is good about you to throw it all away. You'll get over her. You have no other choice," she said.

"I know, but it hurts like hell!"

"I know it does, honey, but you'll see. You will be happy in time, and I know you will make a great doctor. Please believe me."

Brad felt some better for spending time with his mother. On that Sunday afternoon he left for Fayetteville resolved to go on with his plans in spite of his never to have Beth again. He knew, however, that he would always love her.

When Brad got back to Fayetteville, he went directly to the Chemistry Department and looked for the Organic Chemistry grades posted on the bulletin board. Next to his Social Security number, a B was posted. Brad was shocked, because he wasn't sure he had even passed. He was also notified of a very good medical school admission test score.

He had no desire to take part in any fraternity functions nor live in the Kappa Sig house. He kept his small apartment and arranged to keep his job at Wal-Mart, although working various night shifts. With the income from the job and his scholarship money, he was able to get by.

He studied hard in school that fall, and his grades were good. He went to no football games but worked long weekend shifts at Wal-Mart instead.

In October he had interviews for admission to medical school and thought he did fairly well. Brad interviewed with a psychiatrist and then with an associate dean who he assumed was a physician. The psychiatrist asked him questions such as, "Do you ever feel sad? Do you love your parents, Are you happy most of the time?" The dean asked questions like, "Why do you want to be a doctor?" The interviews were not difficult at all, but he was relieved when they were over.

The middle of December he had a three-week break from school for Christmas, but he stayed in Fayetteville to work. He would only go home for a long three-day visit during Christmas Eve and Christmas Day.

When he pulled up in front of his house, Marian came rushing out to the car. "Brad," she stated, "you have a letter from the med school!"

He opened it before going inside. It read:

Dear Mr. Duncan:

It is with great pleasure to announce that you have been accepted for admission to the Freshman Class of 1982. Congratulations. You will need to report on September 6 at 8:00 a.m. for orientation. All tuition and fees will be due at that time.

Further reports will be forthcoming.

Sincerely,

Douglas Lawson, M. D., Dean

University of Arkansas School of Medicine

"Mom, I made it!" he exclaimed.

Marian wiped tears from her eyes and hugged her son. Brad shed a few tears, too. If only Beth could have shared this day with him.

He had not expected to be accepted to medical school until he graduated from the university after his senior year. He only needed twelve hours the next semester to have the ninety needed for early admission, so he would have time to work some day shifts as well as the night shifts already scheduled. Even with that he was afraid there would not be enough money for med school.

"Mom," he said, "I had planned on saving enough money during my senior year for med school. Now I don't know how I can make it."

"Honey, I can help some, but I know how you might get some scholarship money. Do you remember Mrs. Gabbart who went to the Episcopal Church?"

"Yes ma'am," he replied.

"She is very wealthy, and I have heard she gives money for school to kids who agree to be general practice doctors and come back to practice in Fabre's Bluff. Why don't you go see her?"

Brad agreed and phoned Mrs. Gabbart. He was granted an appointment for the day after Christmas.

On the 24th, Brad and Marian attended midnight mass and opened their presents as soon as they got home. They planned to sleep late, have a late breakfast, and then a late afternoon Christmas dinner.

Although tired, Brad's sleep was fitful. He worried about money, but most of all he thought of Beth. Where could she be, what was she doing, what was her husband like and what kind of a job did he have, Did they have children, was she happy, would he ever see her again ran through his brain like a jet plane in a fatal spin.

Christmas Day passed slowly with Brad quiet and Marian trying to cheer him up.

"Brad," she finally said, "you need to get ahold of yourself and cheer up. You'll find a way to get the money for school. And you need to stop mourning over the loss of Beth. Others have lost loved ones and have gotten over it. Look at me- I lost your dad, the only man I ever loved or ever will love. Time will heal if you let it."

"I know," was all he could say.

Mrs. Gabbart lived in the deep woods down a long winding gravel road. As Brad approached her house, he was impressed by how isolated it was and, with all the trees, how cool it must be in the summer.

Mrs. Gabbart answered his knock and invited him in. He was impressed with all the antique furniture, oriental rugs, and fine paintings that gave the great room the appearance of something in a Victorian era movie.

After exchanging pleasantries, Brad came to the point. "Mrs. Gabbart," he said, "I've been accepted to medical school a year earlier than I had thought I would be. I don't have time to accumulate as much money as I'm going to need. I've had scholarships and jobs at Fayetteville, but there is no time for outside jobs while going to med school. Also there are no scholarships. I understand that you have helped med students in the past, and I wonder if you might be willing to help me."

"Young man, what kind of doctor do you want to be and will you come back to Fabre's Bluff to practice?"

"Oh, yes ma'am, I want to go into general practice which is now called family practice, and I definitely plan to come home to practice. I love Fabre's Bluff, and my mother lives here. She's the only family I have."

"Bradley," she said, "I knew your father well. I sold him a lot of timber, and he was always fair with me. He was a good man, and if you turn out to be half the man he was, you will be a fine doctor. I will pay your tuition and buy your books and send you $200 a month. All you will have to do is study hard and promise to come back to Fabre's Bluff to practice."

"Mrs. Gabbart, I really appreciate it. You have my solemn word that Fabre's Bluff will always be my home."

"That is all I need, young man. You're Jim Duncan's son. Your word is as good as gold just like his was."

So Brad now could be at ease for he would be able to afford the cost of med school. He just wished Beth could share it with him.


The spring semester was easy for Brad. All his required courses were out of the way, and he was able to get at least forty hours a week in at Wal-Mart. His grades remained near a four point.

He saw Marie around the campus frequently and often asked her about Beth, but she always said she had heard nothing from her.

Around the first of February Brad heard a knock on his door. It was Marie. She asked if she could come in, and Brad obliged.

After some small talk Marie said, "Brad, I have some news from Beth. She wrote me that she got married over Christmas. She said she was very happy and would be moving to the west coast. She also said that this was the last I would ever hear from her."

Brad tried hard not to show how hurt he was. "Did she give you any idea where she would live or what her married name is? Did she mention me? Who did she marry?"

"She asked me to tell you about the marriage and that she hoped you would be happy and have a good life. That was all she said."

"Can I see the letter?" Brad asked.

"I threw it away," replied Marie. "She said I would never hear from her again, so I saw no need to keep it. To hell with her."

To hell with me, Brad thought. He knew now that there was no hope for him ever finding her. This finally and permanently broke his heart. All he could do was go on living, but he knew he would never be the same.

The rest of the spring semester went by rapidly. Brad was able to make and save a significant amount of money with his longer hours at Wal-Mart. His class work was easy so, in spite of working more hours, he had lots of free time, much of which was spent with Marie Lepanto.

He was beginning to feel comfortable with Marie although he had no romantic or lustful feelings toward her. Not so for Marie who was beginning to again flirt with Brad and obviously had feelings for him.

Toward the end of the school year he asked Marie to go with him on the Kappa Sigma spring outing to Grand Lake in Oklahoma. It was an all day outing with swimming, boat riding and much beer drinking. Brad had a few beers, enough to relax him. Marie had more than enough.

She maneuvered him into a secluded spot, and when she was sure they were alone, she said, "Bradley, sweetie pie, we've been spending a lot of time together. So much time that I'm beginning to fall for you. Beth is out of the picture for good. Why don't you let yourself go and hook up with me? We'd be good for each other. I'd be real good for you, if you get what I mean."

Brad was tempted, maybe because of the beer. He paused and was about ready to agree when he thought again of Beth. "Marie," he said, "you are a good person, an attractive girl, but I can't get Beth out of my head. We might be good together, but Beth would always come between us. It wouldn't be fair to you. You deserve someone who can

love you for you. I would just be taking advantage of you. Please don't
be hurt or mad, but I just can't do it. I doubt I'll ever be able to love
anyone like I should. Beth will always be my cross to bear."

Marie finally gave up on Brad. The rest of the day was
uneventful. A week later Marie was killed in a one car accident. Her
blood alcohol was twice the legal limit.

B rad was distraught over Marie's death and felt at least partially
to blame. If only he could have felt enough affection, if not
love for her, maybe she would still be alive.

He felt so much guilt he went to Father Parks at the Episcopal
Church for help.

After Brad told him the whole story about him, Beth and Marie;
the minister said, "Brad, you were honest with Marie. You didn't love
her but loved another. To marry someone for any reason other than
love is unjust, if not a sin. No one can blame himself for how he
feels, just for how he acts or reacts. One cannot help how he feels or
control how he feels; he can only control how he acts or reacts.

"You did right by Marie. It would have been unfair to her and
unjust to go to her with lust, friendship, sympathy or any emotion
other than love. Stop beating yourself. You did not cause her death
any more than you caused Beth to leave you.

"Go on with your life. Make a good and kind physician. Save
lives, birth babies, comfort the sick. Be obsessed with it. Life will be
good."

Brad felt better. Beth was gone; Marie was gone. Yesterday was
dead, today was alive, tomorrow was only a promise.

When the end of May came and Brad was packing his car getting
ready to leave, he was sad. Brad loved Fayetteville: he loved the color
of leaves there in autumn, the excitement of football season, the
energetic university atmosphere, the cold winters with frequent snow.

His three years there had its highs with Beth, and its lows without Beth. He knew in the years to come, he would remember Fayetteville as the last place he had been with Beth. He would try to remember all those times with her and cherish the memory, for the memories would be all he would ever have of Beth.

He was determined to be content with his life if not happy, but would retain the hope of finding love and happiness again.

The summer was the same as the previous summer- living at home with his mother and working at the asphalt plant.

By September he had the money Mrs. Gabbart had promised as well as over three thousand dollars he had saved. He moved to Little Rock on the first and found a one room garage apartment with bath and rudimentary kitchenette just over a block from the medical school. The room was sparsely furnished with a small dinette, two easy chairs and an end table, all old and worn due to the many medical students having lived there before him. There was a faint odor of oil and gas from the garage below and a musty smell in the room itself. It was to be his home for at least four years. The rent was only fifty dollars a month with water and electricity included. He would have to furnish a phone. Being able to walk to school and back, he needed to spend little money for gas.

The first two days of school were for physicals and indoctrination. One classmate was called back for repeat blood tests, and his roommate kidded him and said, "Don't worry, Lee, it's probably just leukemia." It was, and Lee was to live only long enough to graduate. The roommate felt terrible.

During indoctrination, the speaker said, "Each of you look to the right. Now look to the left. Every one of you has just looked at one person who will flunk out."

That got Brad's attention. He was determined that he would not fail; he would graduate on time and after residency would be a family doctor in Fabre's Bluff.

Many of Brad's classmates were acquaintances from the university. A few were friends and four were fraternity brothers. Soon all one hundred had come to know each other well. The first semester involved only two classes, gross anatomy all morning and biochemistry in the afternoon.

Gross anatomy involved the dissection of human cadavers, four students per cadaver. The bodies supplied by the state were those of unclaimed dead or occasionally a body willed to the school for study. They were lying on row after row of stainless steel tables and were covered by large metal boxes which resembled coffins. The head of each body had been removed prior to the students' arrival. Brad was reminded of old Frankenstein movies the first day of class. Brad's partner was Tom, and the other two partners were John and Charles. The smell of formaldehyde on the students' hands never completely went away, so eating sandwiches at lunch was very unpleasant.

After a few days, Brad had become at least tolerant of the odor. One day after going down the cafeteria line he was looking for a place to sit. He heard a female voice call, "Sit here, Brad, I smelled you coming."

It was Angela Tucker, the girl he had dated briefly at Fayetteville.

"Hi, Angie," he said, "I wondered when I'd run into you."

As he sat at the table, Brad said, "How've you been, Angela? This must be your last year unless you are going for a BSN."

"I've thought about just getting my RN and going to work after this year, but I might stay another year to get the bachelor's degree. What do you think?"

"I'd go for the BSN. It would mean more opportunities for you and in the long run more money."

"That's probably what I'll do. How about you, what are your plans? Where are you living?"

"I've got a little garage apartment a couple of blocks from here. I plan to go into family practice and go back home to Fabre's Bluff to practice."

"That sounds nice," said Angela. "I've lived in Little Rock all my life and am still living with my parents. I'm tired of city life. Maybe I can go to Fabre's Bluff and be your nurse."

Brad was surprised that he liked that idea. She was very attractive and had a good sense of humor. He even felt an attraction to her. For the first time Beth wasn't foremost in his thoughts. Maybe there was some hope for him after all.

The fall semester passed quickly, and Brad found himself looking forward to lunches with Angela. As time passed, he was surprised and pleased that he was actually attracted to her.

Being afraid he might become one of those students looked at during indoctrination who would fail, Brad had devised a strict study schedule. Sunday nights through Thursday nights he would study from 6 p.m. until 10 p.m. no matter whether following days were test days or not. He felt he needed eight hours of sleep to be fresh and clear headed the following day. He would not study Friday nights, Saturdays and Sundays until 6 p.m. Sunday. The days and nights away from the books would be for relaxation or fun activities.

Within a few weeks he was spending his Saturdays with Angela. They went to movies or had picnics or just went on long walks. Sometimes Angela came to his apartment and fixed an evening meal. There was no television so they played gin or listened to music on the phonograph.

In late November the couple took a long walk during an early season snowfall. They laughed as they threw snowballs at each other. They even lay in the snow and made snow angels by waving their arms and legs in the snow. Once, they saw a car go into a spin after braking too fast, but the driver regained control before hitting anything. They ended the walk at Brad's apartment for hot chocolate. Angela sat close to Brad, and soon they were cuddling. Impulsively Brad kissed her, and she responded passionately. That led to lovemaking on the couch, Brad's first time. Angela obviously had prior experience for she had to guide Brad.

Afterwards Brad said, "Angie, believe it or not that was my first time, and it was wonderful."

She replied, "Let's hope it isn't our last." They both laughed, and they both knew it would not be the last.

The next few weeks they were intimate almost weekly. During that time Brad had met her parents, and as Christmas approached he asked her to spend Christmas with him and his mother in Fabre's Bluff.

Brad was beginning to think he was in love with Angela, although he knew it wasn't the same as he had felt for Beth. But Beth was married and gone. He had to get past her and get on with his life. He began to think about marriage. He knew he liked Angela and, if this wasn't love, he told himself he would learn to love her.

Brad and Angela arrived in Fabre's Bluff shortly after noon on the twenty-fourth and went directly to his home. Marian was waiting for them and gave both a welcoming hug.

"I am so excited to meet you, Angela," she said. "Brad has told me so much about you."

"He talks about you all the time, Mrs. Duncan. It's almost like you were his best friend as well as his mother."

"What a compliment from my son," replied Marian.

"Don't let Angie con you, Mom," laughed Brad.

"Now, Bradley," said Angela, "don't let your mother think ill of me."

Marian gave Brad another hug, and they both laughed.

After relaxing for a bit, the three of them rode around town showing Angela all the sights. She was particularly impressed with the river. "I grew up on the Arkansas River," she said. "My dad always had a boat, and from the time I was six or seven, he pulled me on the water skis. The Ouachita is much smaller than the Arkansas, but it is much more beautiful. I would love to live in such a small town as this."

After the sightseeing, while Angela was freshening up for dinner, Brad and Marian had a chance to talk.

"Well, what do you think, Mom?" asked Brad.

"She seems like a nice girl. She's very pretty."

"Is that all you can say?" Brad asked.

"I don't know, honey. You're not getting serious, are you?"

"Mom, I hope you will like her. I'm thinking about asking her to marry me."

"Brad, you haven't said a thing about love."

"Of course I love her," he replied.

"Honey, I want you to think about this very seriously and ask yourself are you in love or in lust. There is a big difference. Love, if nurtured, can last forever; but lust is fleeting. When it is gone and love is not there, a person can be miserable."

It was becoming apparent to Brad that his mother was not too impressed with Angela. Marian seldom smiled around Angela, and when she did it seemed forced. Brad knew just by the look on her face and how rarely she had an animated conversation with Angela that she didn't really care for her. The statement about love and lust confirmed that suspicion for him. "Mother" (he never called her Mother, only Mom), "I don't feel the same about Angie as I feel, felt, about Beth; but Beth is married and out of my life. I've got to go on. I don't want to always be alone. If I don't love Angela as I ought to, I will learn to love her. I do like her a lot."

"Like is important, very important. You must make up your own mind, honey, and I wish you well. I've said all I'm going to say—maybe too much. If you choose to marry Angela, I will treat her as if she were my own daughter. I wish you both all the happiness in the world."

Unbeknownst to either of them, Angela was at the top of the stairs listening to everything.

M idnight Mass that night at the Episcopal Church was very nice and made Brad somewhat homesick. Many friends greeted him, and he introduced Angela to all of them, but she seemed somewhat withdrawn. After the service, she excused herself and went straight to bed in the guest room. Brad, in his old room, was confused and concerned about her quiet demeanor.

The next morning, however, Angela seemed her old self. The three opened presents around the tree. Marian gave Angela a sweater, and Brad gave her an add-a-pearl necklace. She was most appreciative of both gifts.

The rest of the day was uneventful – a typical Christmas Day in small town America.

Early on the twenty-sixth, the couple packed early so they could get an early start back to Little Rock. Marian hugged them both and said, "Brad, study hard and take care of yourself. Angela, it was so good to meet you. I hope to see you again soon. You are always welcome here."

Angela said, "Thank you, Mrs. Duncan. I had a very good time."

"Now I would rather you call me Marian. I feel like we are going to see a lot of each other in the days and years to come."

Brad blushed.

Angela was quiet on the trip to Little Rock. After a short while Brad asked, "Is something bothering you? You're awfully quiet."

"I don't think your mother likes me," she replied rather somberly.

"That's ridiculous; she hardly knows you. Why in the world would you think she dislikes you?" he replied, while knowing that he got the same impression.

"I don't know. It's just a feeling I got," said Angela.

"Well, put it out of your mind. She will like anyone I like or love and anyone who treats me well."

"Are you saying you love me? You have never told me that."

Brad was now placed in a tight spot. He had feelings for Angela but not the feelings he had for Beth. He pulled off at a rest stop, turned off the ignition, and turned so he could look at her.

"Angie, I care about you a lot, more so almost daily. But I have been hurt before, badly hurt. That's why I am hesitant, and that may be what you picked up on from my mother. She knows how hurt I was and, I'm sure, doesn't want to see me hurt again. You need to give me some time to let my fear of being hurt again go away."

"Who was she? Was it Marie? Was it someone I know?"

"No it wasn't Marie, and was no one you know. At least I don't think you knew her, because you were already in nursing school."

"What was her name?"

"Elizabeth," he lied.

"Elizabeth who?"

"Angie, the name doesn't matter. It's over, and over for good. She's married. I don't even know where she lives nor do I care. Now I want you to drop it. I've never asked you about your past romances, and I never will. I'm not going to talk about it anymore. It's a dead issue, once and for all."

Angela knew he was serious and felt it best to change the subject, but she knew that her curiosity would never completely go away.

"Okay," she said, "that's the last I'll ever ask you about it. I do feel better that you've told me."

Brad felt no better, though. He had tried to forget Beth, and now the pain was again present.

The rest of the ten day Christmas holiday found Angela at Brad's apartment every night. They took walks, listened to music, and made love frequently. With each meal she fixed she served wine. Brad would take a small glass, and Angela would have several glasses until the bottle was empty.

The last night of vacation Angela made spaghetti, Brad's favorite meal, and uncorked a bottle of red wine.

"Angie, I'm not much of a drinker. I'd just as soon have Diet Coke as wine. You seem to drink a lot of it. Why don't we do away with the wine, and all alcohol for that matter."

"That's fine with me, Brad," she said, but Brad wasn't sure if she really meant it.

Soon after they finished the meal and while washing the dishes, Angela told him she needed to leave, but she would see him the next night.

Brad said, "Angie, I've got to study. From Sunday night through Thursday night each week I've got to be alone to study. I have to keep up and sure don't want to flunk out. Let's just keep Friday nights, Saturdays and Sundays for us."

Angela agreed, but Brad could tell she didn't like it.

The rest of the spring semester went by fast until late May, two weeks before graduation.

That last Saturday of May, while on a picnic in the park, Angela said, "Brad, I've decided not to stay in school for another year for the BSN. I'm going to graduate next week with an RN and go to work at the University Hospital."

"Why?" asked Brad, " I thought you had your heart set on a BSN."

"Because, I'm pregnant, dammit!"

Brad was shocked. "Are you sure, are you really positive you are?"

"I'm sure the tests were positive all three times I took them."

"But you were on the pill," he almost shouted.

"You ought to know the pill isn't one hundred percent. I could have missed one, I don't know. I'm only eight weeks. I guess I could get an abortion."

"No you can't," replied Brad. "It's my baby too, and I will not have it killed. We'll just get married and have the baby. We'll get a bigger apartment. I'll work all summer in Fabre's Bluff. I can live with Mom, and you can have the baby here in Little Rock and stay with your parents until you can go to work. I'll come home each weekend. It will work out fine."

"But you don't love me," she protested.

"Of course I do. You being the mother of my child will make me love you even more."

So the decision was made. They would be married and have a child. Now he would truly have to put Beth out of his mind. If only he could!

Angela didn't want to go through premarital counseling by a minister, so the couple had a civil ceremony at the Pulaski County Courthouse with only Marian and her parents present. The ceremony was performed by a Justice of the Peace in a small anteroom off the main courtroom. The only witness was a female clerk. The civil ceremony lasted less than five minutes. During the ceremony, Brad was thinking that this would not be the kind of wedding he would have had with Beth. After a two day honeymoon in Hot Springs, they spent the last three weeks of the semester in Brad's small apartment.

On June the sixth, Angela went through the graduation

ceremony, was capped and pinned. All she needed to be able to work as an RN was to take and pass the state nursing board exam. They kept the apartment but she stayed with her parents, and Brad moved to Marian's house in Fabre's Bluff and began his annual summer job at the asphalt plant. Angela studied for the board exam, took it toward the end of the month, and passed. She decided to take the rest of the summer off and wait until Brad moved back to Little Rock to go to work at the University Hospital.

Brad was bothered by that decision since he knew they would need all the money either of them could make for living expenses. He did not protest due to his wife's pregnancy, but would just try to get all the overtime he could that summer.

After the first two weeks in Fabre's Bluff, Brad got a phone call from Mrs. Gabbart. "Brad," she said, "could you come to my home Sunday to visit? I would prefer you come alone."

"Of course I can, Mrs. Gabbart. What time would you like me to come?"

"Would two o'clock be convenient for you?" she replied.

"That will be fine, Ma'am. I'll see you then," said Brad.

Brad was somewhat bothered by the call, but he showed up and knocked on her door at precisely two o'clock.

"Come in young man," said Mrs. Gabbart as she opened the door. "You are exactly on time. I like that in a person."

"Thank you Ma'am," he said as he entered the foyer.

She led him into the sitting room and motioned for him to sit down.

After inquiring if Brad would like tea, which he declined, she got to the point. "Brad, I understand you have married. That concerns me a bit since I know how young women are who have been brought up in the city. I fear that your bride will not want to live in Fabre's Bluff and will influence you to live and practice in Little Rock."

Brad started to speak but was stopped by the raised hand of the old lady.

"Young man, I want your assurance that you will be true to your word and will practice here after your graduation and internship. I want you to keep your commitment for at least five years."

"Mrs. Gabbart, you have no cause for alarm. My dream has been always to practice in Fabre's Bluff. And not for just five years, I plan to live in this town all my life and raise my children here. I love this place. It will always be home. In less than three years I will graduate and then will take a three year Family Practice residency and then spend the rest of my life right here. That is a solemn promise."

"But what about your wife?" she asked.

"Angela knows my plan and she has agreed to it. She will like it here and will work as a nurse in my office."

"Young man, you let her work at the hospital and not in your office. An old country doctor once said, 'Never hug your nurse or hire your wife', and that is good advice."

The summer was hot and humid but passed quickly. Each workday began at seven and ended at six with one dump truck after another either coming or going. Each truck had to be weighed empty as it entered and full as it exited, then the cost was computed and billed to its owner. Brad kept a large Thermos of ice water. His lunch was usually a cheese sandwich. The restroom was a bushy tree behind the weight shack. Brad was very tired after the ten hour days. Angela came to Fabre's Bluff the few weekends Brad didn't go to Little Rock, but she seldom visited with Marian.

One morning in early August, Brad followed Marian outside as she was leaving for work. He could sense something was bothering her. "Mom, what is it? I can tell you've got something on your mind."

"Brad, honey, I don't think Angela is pregnant."

"Why in the world would you think that?"

"I know how a woman looks and feels in the first few months," replied Marian. "Angela hasn't had any morning sickness as far as I can tell. She sleeps late, and when she finally gets up she has a really big appetite. Pregnant women just don't eat that much at breakfast. She has gained no weight, but most of all I found evidence of menstruation in the garbage can. When I did, I looked through the can and found much more evidence, if you know what I mean."

"Why would she fake a pregnancy, Mom? Maybe she miscarried and is in denial or something."

"Brad, think about it. Would you have married her had she not been pregnant?"

"No! At least not now – maybe someday. Well I'll be damned," he exclaimed.

That night when he and Angela were alone Brad said, "Angie, I know you're not pregnant. I found evidence of menstruation in our garbage can, and I know Mom has gone through menopause."

Angela was quiet. She sat for a moment, then stood and walked around the room. She stopped in front of the window, looking blankly into the distance. When she finally turned to face Brad, she avoided direct eye contact.

When she finally spoke she said, "I aborted spontaneously six or seven weeks ago. I just didn't have the heart to tell you."

"Did you go to a doctor?"

"There was no need. It was complete and in a tiny sac. There was very little bleeding, and I have since had a normal period."

"I am so sorry," said Brad. "You should have told me. I know you were disappointed."

"No I wasn't. Actually I was glad. I didn't want a baby. It would interfere with my career and with my life. I might as well tell you now. I don't ever want children. I'd be a terrible mother, and I will not get pregnant again."

Brad was quite angry but said nothing. He just walked out of the room, out of the house, and into the warm night.

The rest of August went by in a blur. The couple had little to say to each other the weekends they were together, and Marian kept her distance. Finally he packed and went back to Little Rock. They found a three room apartment within walking distance to the medical school and hospital.

Brad was in his sophomore year, the last pre-clinical year. His hours were seven to five with weekends off. Angela, having passed her licensing exam, went to work on the internal medicine wing working the three to eleven shift. She had every other weekend off. This arrangement served them both fine as they weren't as close as most young couples.

The years went by fast, and during Brad's senior year, he was called to the hospital administrator's office. When he arrived, he found Angela and the Director of Nurses waiting with Mr. Dickson, the administrator.

Mr. Dickson motioned for Brad to take a seat and then said, "Mr. Duncan, a shortage of codeine has been detected on the wing. Mrs. Duncan has signed off on the incorrect count. She has refused a drug screen. You need to talk to her. If she won't submit to the screen, she will be terminated. The incident will be reported to the nursing board. If she takes the screen and it is positive, she will be suspended and the matter turned over to the board. You need to talk with her. We will leave and give you five minutes."

After the two officials left, Brad asked, "Angela, did you take the drugs?"

"No."

"Did you divert them?"

"No," she said emphatically. "I have no idea what happened to them. Someone else may have taken them. I didn't!"

"Well then, why didn't you take the drug screen?"

"I don't know," she replied. "It just pisses me off that they would suspect me. It's just a matter of principle."

"You don't have a choice. Take the drug screen. If you haven't taken the drugs, it will be negative."

"Okay," she said, I'll take it, but I don't like it."

She took the test, and it came back negative but positive for a mild tranquilizer for which she had a valid prescription. Brad had no idea she was on tranquilizers.

Since there was no proof Angela had diverted the medication, she was not terminated. She was, however, put on probation for a year and was not allowed to handle narcotics unsupervised for that year.

There were no more problems with drug counts, but Brad

remained mildly suspicious.

Late in his senior year, Brad found out that he had been accepted by the university to do his family practice residency there. He and Angela could remain in Little Rock for the next three years, and she could keep her job. With her pay and his small stipend, they could live fairly well. They knew they had to continue to be very frugal, however. During medical school they had only her income and whatever he could save from summer jobs. Their one big meal each day was taken at the University Hospital cafeteria. At home, they had lots of bologna sandwiches. Due to his studies and Angela's work schedule, they were able to find time for a meal out and a movie only about once a month. Now, Brad's residence and her work schedule would probably not even allow that. Their one splurge was a small black and white television for the apartment.

In early June he graduated with BSM and MD degrees. A week later he took the State Medical Board and passed. So by July first, he was a physician fully licensed by the State of Arkansas. All that separated him from his dream of practicing medicine in Fabre's Bluff was three years of residency training.

Residency required very long hours with six month rotations in internal medicine, pediatrics, obstetrics, and surgery. His third year would be rotations of his choice. He and Angela would have less time together for the three years due to his long hours seven days a week and her forty hour weekly work schedule.

On the very first night of his residency an incident occurred that would remain a joke for the next three years.

He was on the internal medicine rotation and on call. Being on call he was required to stay at the hospital for twenty four hours. Shortly after midnight he was called to a patient's room. When he arrived, he found two nurses and an orderly standing by the bed of an obviously dead patient.

"This man is dead," Brad said. "What do you need me for?"

"Doctor," said the older nurse, "we need you to pronounce him dead."

During medical school Brad had learned about all kinds of exotic diseases, but nothing about pronouncing people dead. Rather than ask a nurse what to do he just placed his left hand on the patient's head, raised his right hand, and said, "I pronounce thee dead!"

His first rotation was internal medicine, and he worked trying to develop a bedside manner. Whenever he entered a female patient's room on rounds, he would quickly size her up and say, "Hello ma'am, I'm Dr. Duncan." If he thought she was thirty five he would say, "How old are you, about twenty eight?"

The patient would say, "No, I'm thirty five," and the ice would be broken.

That practice abruptly ended when he entered a woman's room who he thought looked about fifty. "How old are you, about forty?" he asked.

She looked shocked and said, "No, I'm twenty nine!"

He liked his six months on internal medicine; but he found his next rotation, pediatrics, a real joy. He loved the little children, particularly the babies.

Before the six month rotation was over he had almost decided to go into pediatrics. However, his next rotation was obstetrics; and that is where he found his real talent. Within a short period of time he became quite adept at delivering babies. He learned to use outlet forceps and became expert at it.

The call rotation on obstetrics was twenty four hours on and twenty four off. He had work in the clinics five days a week so that he only got eight to ten hours of sleep every forty eight hours. That left little time for him to spend with Angela, but neither seemed to mind.

The only way Brad could do both pediatrics and obstetrics would be to go into family practice, so he remained dedicated to his three year commitment to the family practice residency.

Thе shorter rotations gave Brad more free time, so he and
Angela had more time together.

Over dinner one evening in the beginning of Brad's third and
last year of residency, Angela said, "Brad, I like my job at the med
center, and I like living in Little Rock. I don't want to move to Fabre's
Bluff. You can do just as well here in Little Rock and can probably
work less hard and make more money too. Let's stay here."

"No, Angie," he said. "My goal and desire has always been to be
a doctor and live and practice in Fabre's Bluff. And anyway, I gave
my word to Mrs. Gabbart that I would do just that. She financed me
based on that word. I'll not go back on it."

"What can she do if you don't go back there? You have no
contract. There is nothing that binds you to go there."

"My word binds me, but more than that, my desire to live in
Fabre's Bluff and my love of the place binds me. That is where I will
live and practice with or without you. If you don't want to go there
with me, I'll not contest your petition for divorce."

That was the first ever mention of divorce by either of them.

Angela was stunned. She pivoted and took a few brisk steps away
from him, then did an about face and focused a ferocious scowl at
him. After a short pause she said, "No, I'll go. After helping pay your
way through medical school, I'm not about to give up riding on the
gravy train."

Brad knew then that he could never really love Angela as a man
should love his wife. But he was obligated to her. He had married
her. He would continue to be her husband in every way—even in bed.
Maybe he was in lust instead of in love after all.

Halfway through Brad's third year he got an offer to come into
practice with Dr. James Jackson and Dr. Donald Glover. Dr. Jackson

had been the Duncan family's doctor for many years. He was fifty five, and Don Glover was ten years his junior.

Jim was wanting to give up obstetrics, so Don and Brad would deliver all the babies. The three would share medical call, and Don and Brad would be on obstetrical call every other night. That suited Brad fine.

In July the couple moved to Fabre's Bluff and settled into a fairly new three bedroom house close to the river and about a mile from Marian's home.

Angela got a job on the medical wing but was disappointed she couldn't work in Brad's office. The Jackson-Glover Clinic had a rule that wives could not work in the clinic. Brad's nurse, Edith, was a licensed practical nurse in her mid thirties. She was a very kind and gentle woman who was very efficient and well liked by his patients.

The first four months were pleasant and uneventful for both Brad and Angela until early November.

Brad had Wednesday afternoons off, and when he got home at noon, Angela asked him to sit down.

"We need to talk," she said.

"Okay, what about?" he replied.

"I'm pregnant, that's what," she said rather too forcefully.

Brad was delighted but tried not to show it. "How do you know?" he asked.

"I've just missed my second period, I'm getting nauseated, and my breasts are swollen and tender. I've taken three pregnancy tests, and all are positive.

"Well, I'll be," said Brad. "We're gonna have a baby."

"Brad, I told you I never want children. I meant it then, and I mean it now. I want an abortion and then no more sex or you have a vasectomy."

Brad was beginning to feel hate for her for the first time, but he remained calm. "No abortion, Angie, I mean it. If you do anything to cause an abortion, we're through. No more sex is okay by me, but we will have this baby.

"Now I'll tell you what I'll do. I have a patient named Etta Mae Brown. She is a thirty-something year old widow, a black lady, who is very kind and a really good person. She is out of work since the family she worked for a number of years has moved. She does housework, is a good cook and a great nanny. I'll hire her to keep house and take care of the baby. I'll take care of it on the weekends and at night."

"But what about when you have to deliver a baby at night?"

"I'll phone her to come over and pay her extra."

"Does she drive?"

"Hell, I'll buy her a car! It will work out. No, we are going to have this baby. It will be our only one. If you don't want it, fine, but it will be mine. Dammit, I mean it. I'm as serious as a heart attack.

"Whenever Etta Mae can't help, Mom will. Now Angela, I mean it. If you do away with this baby, we are through!"

"Okay, Brad, you'll get your baby; but this will be the only one, and you damn well better keep your promise."

"I'll keep the promises, every one of them. You can put that in the bank!"

The next day Brad phoned Etta Mae and asked her to come to his office to talk. He also made an appointment for Angela to see Don Glover for initial prenatal care after fully explaining the situation to Don.

Etta Mae Brown was in her late thirties, tall, heavy-set, and had medium brown skin. She had a very pretty face that made her look younger than she was. Her smile was most engaging, and her demeanor was relaxed and pleasant.

She was escorted into Brad's main office and invited to sit. Edith said, "Make yourself comfortable, Etta Mae. Dr. Duncan will be in very soon."

Etta Mae took a seat in a soft leather chair next to Brad's large cluttered desk. She noticed pictures of wildlife on the walls and a framed photograph of his parents on his desk. She was somewhat surprised to see no picture of a wife.

Within a few minutes Brad walked in, smiled at Etta Mae, and took a seat beside her rather than behind his desk.

"Thanks for coming, Mrs. Brown," he said.

"Why, you're welcome, Dr. Duncan. What can I do for you?"

"You can go to work for me as a housekeeper, but you may not want to after you hear me out," he said.

"Oh, I doubt that, Doctor. What do you need me to do?"

"I'm gonna be up front and honest with you, Mrs. Brown."

"Call me Etta Mae, please, Doctor. Mrs. Brown sounds too high fallutin."

"Okay, Etta Mae," he said. "My wife is going on three months pregnant. She is not happy, and I doubt she ever will be. She doesn't want this baby, but I do. We've had some words about it. I get along with her okay, but she may be a little hard for you to get along with.

"She will probably be at least cordial with you, because she will want you to have total care of the baby, keep up the house and maybe even cook a little," he explained.

"I can do that, Doctor. I love little babies and growin' children too. I bet we can get along okay. Lord knows I've worked for some mighty cranky women in my time and got along fine with them."

"Now, Etta Mae, I'll need you to come to work at seven and stay till I get home, usually by six. I have Wednesday afternoons off, so you can be off then. Sometimes I may have to ask you to come at night when I have to go deliver a baby, at least when my child is a baby and not sleeping all night. I may need you some on weekends. I'll pay you fifty a week, extra for weekends, and extra when you have to come at night."

"That'll be fine, but I got to be off for church on Sundays," she said.

"That will be okay. If I need someone on Sunday, my mother can come. Do you drive?"

"Yes sir, but I don't have a car."

"That's okay. I've already talked to the Buick dealer. He has a used Ford, late model, that I will buy for you. I'll buy all your gas, pay the insurance and all, and you can use it as if it were your own. How does that sound?"

"Just fine. When do you want me to start to work?"

"How about Wednesday afternoon about one o'clock? I'll be off then and can introduce you to my wife and be there if you need anything."

"Doctor Duncan, we've got a deal," Etta Mae said.

As they stood and headed to the door, he took her hand in his and patted the back of it with his left hand. "Etta Mae, I appreciate this. You're going to be a life-saver. I know my baby will love you. I'll come by your house with your car after work this evening, and you can drive me home."

"Thanks, Doctor," she said as they parted. She was mildly bothered by his always referring to the unborn child as his baby rather than as their baby.

That evening Brad told Angela he had hired Etta Mae, and Angela was neither glad nor mad about it but was indifferent. She just shrugged her shoulders, said nothing, but turned and walked away.

After a while she asked, "Is she clean?"

"Of course she is," replied Brad, rather too forcefully.

"I didn't mean to make you mad, Bradley. I just want to be sure I don't have to be around here all day with a nigger woman who smells bad."

"Now wait a minute, Angela. I'll not have you refer to her that way. You can say she's black or colored or African American, but you'd better not ever call her a nigger. I'd rather think of her as just a woman not really different from you or me. She is a kind and gentle lady and is to be treated as such. I mean it!" he said, trying hard to keep his voice down.

"I didn't mean to get your dander up. I just wanted to make sure she was clean."

"Well, she is!" he exclaimed, as he left her and went into the den. He needed a drink, a stiff one, but he was on call so he couldn't.

At precisely one o'clock on Wednesday, Etta Mae drove up in the ten year old Ford that Brad had given her, its paint now faded and its windshield now cracked. She walked up the sidewalk briskly with her head held high and rang the doorbell.

Brad got out of his chair and looked at Angela. Expressionless, Angela avoided eye contact.

"Hello, Etta Mae, come in," he said. "Etta Mae, this is my wife, Angela. Angela, this is Etta Mae Brown."

"How do, Miz Duncan."

"Hello, Etta Me, it was good of you to come. I'm so happy you're going to work for us."

Brad was stunned at how pleasant Angela was. It had been weeks since he had seen her smile or speak with such a pleasant tone.

Angela took over with Etta Mae, showed her around the house, and in a very nice way told her what her duties were to be. She would start work the following Monday. Angela even gave her a key to the house since she would be at work at the hospital that day on the seven to three shift.

As Brad walked Etta Mae to the car she said, "We gonna do okay, Doctor."

Brad was pleased but more relieved than pleased. When he went back in, Angela looked at him, said, "She'll do," and went into her room and closed the door.

The next two months went by fairly uneventfully. Angela worked Monday through Friday on the seven to three shift. Brad's practice was growing almost daily, and Etta Mae was enjoying her job in the Duncan home.

At the mid-stage of the pregnancy, Angela went in for an ultrasound. While she was in Dr. Glover's examining room, Don approached Brad in the hall. "Brad," he said, "You'd better come with me. You need to be with Angela when I tell her about the ultrasound."

"Is something wrong?" Brad asked, rather urgently.

"No, but she has twins."

"Oh, my God," exclaimed Brad. "She didn't want one baby. I

don't know what she'll do when you tell her there are two."

"I know," said Don, "that's why I want you with me."

Both men were anxious when they entered the examination room.

"What's wrong?" Angela asked, when she saw Brad. "Is something wrong with the baby?"

"No, nothing like that," said Don. "Brace yourself, Angie, you're carrying twins."

Angela just stared at Brad but said nothing.

"I can't be sure," said Don, "but I think they're a boy and a girl."

"Well, I guess Brad and Etta Mae are gonna have their hands full," was all she said.

Brad said, "It'll be fine, Angie. I've got to get back to work. I'll see you at home at noon."

Angela said nothing as the two men left the room, but in a few minutes she rushed into Brad's office and slammed the door. "Dammit, Brad, look what you've got me into. Two damned babies. You wouldn't let me have an abortion and now it's too late."

"Angela, I know you're mad, and I'm sorry you feel the way you do. But you'd better not do anything to damage these babies. Just have them, and I'll take over. You won't have to do a thing." His feelings at the point were bordering on hate.

"I'll have them alright, but you and Etta Mae and your mother better do what you said and raise them. I don't know if I'll even hang around in this damn town." Then she stormed out the same way she stormed in.

The next few months were unremarkable. The pregnancy was uneventful and there were no more outbursts. Angela neither talked nor complained about her pregnancy. When Brad suggested they consider names for the babies, she just shrugged her shoulders and said, "Whatever. I could care less."

Finally, two weeks prior to term, she had the babies by Caesarian section. The boy weighed a little over six pounds, and the girl almost six. The boy was nineteen inches long and the girl was eighteen. Both were chubby and had a fair amount of hair, indications that they were near term if not full term. Brad thought they were the most beautiful babies he had ever seen.

After she awoke from the anesthetic, Brad and a nurse brought the babies in for her to hold. She said, "I don't want to hold them. Take them back to the nursery."

The next day Brad visited her in her room. "Angie," he said, "we've got to name them. Do you have any preferences?"

"Suit yourself. I don't care what you name them. They're your babies."

"I'd like to name the boy Bradley Andrew, Jr., and call him Brad. I'd like to name the girl Beth. I think Brad and Beth sound good for twins."

"Why don't you give the girl a more formal name like Elizabeth and call her Beth?"

"I like Beth," was all he could think of to say.

"I don't care. Do whatever you want."

So he named them Beth and Bradley Andrew, Jr. At last he had a Beth.


Over the next few months the twins thrived. By the time they were three months old they had doubled their birth weights and were on schedule in their social development.

Brad doted on them, Marian was thrilled with them, Etta Mae loved them; but Angela remained indifferent.

Brad had suggested several times to Angela that she seek treatment for postnatal depression, but her response was always that she was not depressed but was unhappy.

"Do you love the kids?" Brad asked her once.

"I don't know," she said. "I care about them and want them to do well, but I wish I'd never had them. You knew I didn't want kids. Now I've got two, and I don't think I can handle it. Thank God for

Etta Mae. I know you're gonna be a great father and Marian a super grandmother, but I was never meant to be a mother. I don't like it, and I don't like this jerk-water town."

Brad just gave up on Angela. He would stay married to her because he had promised for better or worse, but he knew the marriage was a sham. He vowed to himself that he would raise these children right, whatever it took.

The months and years passed, and the twins thrived. Etta Mae became almost a mother figure; and Marian, who they called Nanny, was a wonderful grandmother.

When Brad, Jr. and Beth were almost three, Brad got a call from the hospital administrator's secretary asking him to come to the office at once. He dropped what he was doing and did as he was requested to do.

When he got to the office, the secretary told him to go on in. He knocked, didn't wait for the door to be opened for him, opened the door and went in.

The administrator, Mr. Alexander, was sitting behind his desk; and Angela was sitting on the couch.

"Take a seat, Doctor, we've got a problem."

Brad looked at Angela, who looked away, and took a seat in a chair facing the desk.

"Dr. Duncan, we have a significant shortage of hydrocodone that Mrs. Duncan was responsible for. She has admitted diverting the drugs for her own use. I have terminated her and must report this to the state board of nursing. In deference to you, I will not press charges. I hope she will get treatment for her dependency."

Brad was shocked. After a pause, he said, "Thank you, Mr. Alexander. Come on, Angela, I'll take you home."

They rode home in silence, and when they arrived, Brad parked the car and said, "Don't get out, Angie, we need to talk."

"There's really nothing to say," said Angela.

"Yes there is. You obviously have a problem. I want you to go into treatment at the Drug and Alcohol Center in Shreveport. You need help with drugs and also I think you need psychiatric help."

"Okay, Brad, I'll do whatever you say. But I'm tired. Just leave me alone and let me be by myself and sleep on it. I promise that tomorrow I'll go wherever you say."

"I don't feel right leaving you alone," he said.

"Oh, hell, Brad, I'm not gonna do anything stupid. I just want to be alone to sort things out. I'll be okay. Just give me a little space."

They had a quick supper fixed by Etta Mae, and when Angela rose to go to the bedroom she said, "Brad, I'll see you in the morning. Make whatever calls you need to make. I'll be ready to go into treatment tomorrow. If you ever loved me, just let me have tonight alone and in peace."

She went into her room, closed the door, and never once looked at her children.

The next morning Brad called his answering service and asked to have his schedule for the rest of the week cleared.

Etta Mae arrived at seven and started breakfast. He explained the situation to her and told her he might need her to stay late for several nights.

When breakfast was ready, the aroma of fresh coffee and smoked bacon followed Brad to Angela's door. Brad knocked but got no answer. He opened the door and entered the room. Angela was in bed, and an empty medicine bottle was on the floor. He looked again and realized she was dead. A note was on the bedside table.

For a few moments Brad just sat on the bed beside her. He had never considered that she might kill herself, and he was angry at himself for not thinking of it.

Finally he picked up the note and read it. It said:

*Brad,*
 *I loved you once. I don't know what happened*
*to that love, but somewhere along the way it died. I suspect you*
*never really loved me, but I can't be sure.*
*You know, I'm sure, that I tricked you into marrying me.*

*I wasn't pregnant. I'm ashamed of that and sorry for it.*
*I've abused drugs for years, even at the med center when*
*I finally took the drug test. The only time I didn't use drugs was*
*when I was pregnant with the twins. I didn't want to raise a child,*
*much less a drug damaged kid.*

*This is the only way out for me. You have every right to*
*hate me, but by doing this I am actually doing you a favor. Think*
*about it.*

*Don't blame yourself for this. It's all my fault.*

*Be happy and love the twins as I know you can. I couldn't.*
*Goodbye,*
*Angela*

After the funeral, life in the Duncan household was peaceful and settled into a routine. Etta Mae was there five and a half days a week, off only on Wednesday afternoons, Brad's afternoon off.

Brad gave up his obstetrical practice so he could be with the twins every night. Marian was there with the three of them almost every weekend.

Little Brad and Beth went to pre-school at four and kindergarten at five.

The weekend before the twins were to start the first grade, Marian took them to buy school clothes and ran other errands for Brad.

After a late dinner Sunday night and the children were put to bed, Brad and his mother sat on the porch. They were quiet for a while, and then Marian asked her son why he didn't start to date.

"Mom, it would lead to nothing. You asked me once if I were in love or in lust. It was lust, pure and simple; and marrying for lust wasn't fair to Angela."

"I have always loved Beth – the first Beth, not my little girl, although I love her dearly as I do Brad– and I can't forget her. Even in the middle of the night with Angela, I was thinking of Beth and wishing it was her with me. I'll never get over her; I know it. I'm not going to take the chance of cheating someone else. You said yourself that a person should only marry for love, and I can't have Beth. So I have no intention of dating, or marrying, again. If I can't have the woman I love, I choose to have no one."

Marian was silent, for she had no idea what to say.

"And remember once," Brad went on, "when you quoted a poem and said I would have hope, sweet hope, and be together again with Beth? We'll, I've read that poem – I've read it many times. It said 'in the hereafter some sweet hope lies deeply buried from human eyes'. Well, I want Beth in this life, and I can't have her. She's married and probably has several children. And if there is a hereafter, I'm sure she will want to be with her husband and her kids. There would be no place for me. So there is no sweet hope for me."

Early the next morning the kids were almost too excited about starting first grade to eat their breakfast.

Brad said, "Relax, kiddos. We'll be on time. First grade is not much different from kindergarten. It'll be fun."

"We know," said Beth. "We just don't want to be late. Hurry up, Daddy."

"We'll be on time; that's a promise," replied Brad.

When all three finished their breakfast, Little Brad and Beth ran to Etta Mae and gave her a hug.

Brad noticed a tear in her eye when she said, "You kids go on now with your daddy. You'll have fun at school. I'll pick you up when school lets out."

The children were excited all the way to school, but when they arrived, they became quiet and withdrawn. Brad thought they were just nervous. He uncoupled their car seat harnesses and helped them out of the car. He took a small hand in each of his hands and began the walk to the main entrance. They passed many excited first graders all standing with their mothers.

Brad took them to their assigned room, said hello to their teacher, gave each a hug, and left.

That afternoon Etta Mae was waiting at the curb when the children came out. When they got in the car, Beth was crying.

"What's the matter, child?"

Beth said nothing, but Brad said, "She's upset 'cause some of the kids teased us because we didn't have a mama to bring us to school, and they all did."

Etta Mae became angry but tried hard not to show it. "You tell those kids you got a mama, but she is in heaven with Jesus. Her and Jesus is watchin' over you all, and Jesus don't like teasin' about things like that."

That seemed to satisfy Beth, and she stopped crying.

Finally she spoke. "Why did she go to be with Jesus when we were so little, Etta Mae? We needed her here to take care of us."

"Well, child, let me tell you. Your mama was sick, too sick to take care of you. She couldn't get well. So Jesus knew she could watch over you best in heaven with Him to help her. He knew me and your daddy and Nanny could take care of you here. So He took her to heaven where she wouldn't be sick no more and could watch over you. He knew me and your daddy and Nanny would do right, and you'd be okay."

"Oh," was all each of them could say, but Etta Mae knew they were satisfied.

Most days after school when Etta Mae picked the twins up at school, she took them to her house for a while prior to taking them home. The children enjoyed those times. They felt at peace there unlike the vague memories they had of conflicts at home. They had few memories of their mother, but something about those memories was uncomfortable to them.

Etta Mae's house was small and comfortable and had a smell about it different from their house, but very pleasant to them. Especially pleasant was the smell when Etta Mae cooked her sweet potato pie for the Duncan family. The kids watched her every move and excitedly awaited the opportunity to lick the pan.

As they grew older, they noticed there were no white people in Etta Mae's neighborhood, only black. They were confused about that and also why there were no black people in their neighborhood. That caused Beth to wonder why some people were darker-skinned than others. She asked her brother why, and all he could say was, "I don't know," as he went about playing with the toys Etta Mae had for them.

Finally she asked, "Etta Mae, why is your skin brown and mine is light colored? Why are all the people around here dark and around my house they're light colored?"

"Well, I'll tell you, child. Way back long ago in Bible time, God made people, and they was all alike. All of 'em had light tan skin. Now as there got to be more and more people, some of 'em went south to Africa and some of 'em went north where it was cold."

Both children listened intently.

She went on, "Now you know how in the summertime you play in the sprinklers and get sunburned. Then you get tan when the sunburn heals, and if you get lots of sun you get real tan. Well, them people who went to Africa where it's real hot kept gettin' so much sun that they just stayed dark, and them that went north didn't get much sun so they got lighter. That's how it came about that some of us is dark-skinned and some is light-skinned.

"We're all the same in God's eyes, though. It's just that dark-skinned people is poorer than light-skinned people. That's another story, though, and you all is too young for that now."

The next day Brad came home at noon as he had the afternoon off. Etta Mae greeted him and said, "Dr. Duncan, the twins are asking me all kinds of questions. Some I don't know how to answer. What do you want me to do about answering them?"

"Just answer them truthfully as best you can. If you don't know the answer, just say you don't know. That's what I do," he replied.

"Okay, I'll do my best," she said.

"Etta Mae, how old are you?" Brad asked.

"Thirty nine."

"Well, that's three years older than I. We need to come to an understanding about something."

Uh oh, she thought.

Brad went on, "Etta Mae, you're older than me and pretty much part of my family. I trust you with my children and everything else I have. I want you to stop calling me Dr. Duncan. Call me Brad. That's my name."

"Oh, no sir," she said, "I can't do that."

"Well, if you don't, I'm gonna call you Mrs. Brown. I mean it. I'm Dr. Duncan at the office and the hospital. I want to be Brad at home."

"I tell you what – I got one Brad, and Lord knows he's enough. Two's too many. How 'bout I just call you Doc."

"Okay," he said. "That'll be fine. I just don't want you to be so damned formal all the time."

Years passed, and the twins grew and thrived. Beth filled out and became a beautiful teenager. She was active in drama class, and was quite popular. In her first play in drama class, Beth was given the title role in The Song of Bernadette. Brad told her she should be in Hollywood, and Marian agreed. Many friends were in and out of the Duncan home, much to the delight of her father.

Brad was quieter than his sister and more studious. Math was his favorite subject. He made an A+ in Algebra and an A in geometry. He showed natural leadership on both his football and basketball teams, where he could always be found encouraging struggling teammates. He played quarterback on the football team and forward on the basketball team. In his junior year, he was elected captain of the football team, an honor that had never before gone to anyone not a senior.

One night when the twins were in the eleventh grade, Brad came home around midnight. The house was a mess. Obviously there had been a party, and a wild one at that. Empty beer bottles were everywhere. Partially eaten pizza littered tables and chairs. Two lamps were overturned and one of them was broken. Paper plates and wadded napkins littered the carpet. The overwhelming odor was of vomit.

The next morning, being Saturday, he let the kids sleep in. His son came into the kitchen first. Brad was having his coffee. Etta Mae was sitting with him at the table.

"Go get your sister and bring her down now," he calmly said.

The boy did as he was told, and shortly he came back with his sister who was rubbing sleep out of her eyes.

"Sit down," he said, and they complied.

"Don't say a word— just listen," he began. "I can't tell you how disappointed I am in you two."

"Dad – " Beth started.

"Hush," he said. "Just listen. You've broken the law having alcohol in the house. You are under aged. That will not happen again. When you're legally of age if you choose to drink that is your right. It is illegal now and will not be tolerated. I hope if you do drink when you're grown, it will be in moderation – in other words, socially. Drinking to get drunk is dangerous and stupid. I'll not put up with it.

"I imagine you are both wondering what I'm going to do about last night. Well, I'll tell you. Your cars will be parked for a month. You are to spend this weekend cleaning up the mess you and your buddies made.

"I'll drive you to school every day for the rest of this semester— about six weeks, I think. Etta Mae will pick you up after school, Beth, and after ball practice, Brad.

"That is every day of the week except Mondays. On the next six Mondays you will be picked up by a deputy sheriff in his patrol car. He will take you to the county jail where Sheriff Gardner has agreed to let you clean up the drunk tank. I mean all the vomit and whatever else is on the floor. That's your punishment."

"Aw, Dad," said Brad. Beth just looked down at her feet.

"That's it," said their father. "If anything like this happens again, it'll be worse."

Etta Mae had to turn away so that the twins couldn't see her grin.

Each Monday the twins were picked up in a patrol car and taken to the jail. Friends laughed and taunted them as they walked to the car. They were thoroughly embarrassed, which is what their father had expected.

At the dinner table the second Monday of their punishment, Beth spoke first. "Daddy," she said, "could at least Etta Mae pick us up and take us to the jail? It's terrible the way we're getting teased. It's almost as bad as cleaning the drunk tank."

"It's worse!" exclaimed her brother.

"Okay, kiddos," said Brad. "I'm gonna give in just this once. Etta Mae can pick you up. You don't have to ride in the patrol car."

"Oh, thanks, Daddy! How about cutting short the clean-up job?" Beth asked.

"Don't push your luck, kids. Tell me about the clean-up job."

"It's terrible," said Beth. "There's puke and worse stuff on the floor. The men still there get moved into another cell while we're cleaning up. They're dirty and repulsive."

"They stink. The whole jail stinks," was all Brad, Jr. would say.

"One man even messed in his pants," said Beth. "Not number one – number two!"

"Let me ask you both something," said Brad. "Do you know how disappointed in you I am?"

Both said, "Yes sir," as the boy looked down at the floor, and his sister shed a tear.

"Have you learned a lesson and will anything like this happen again? Can I begin to trust you again?"

"Yes sir," said Beth.

"How about you, Brad?" his father asked.

"Dad, I've let you down. I'm sorry and ashamed about that. I'm sorry about it. You trusted us and I guess we betrayed that trust. It was my idea. Beth had nothing to do with it. Please let her off. She doesn't need to be in that filthy jail and see all that crap and stuff. I'll do the full six weeks, but let her off."

"I'm gonna let you both off, but you don't get your cars back for two more weeks. Etta Mae won't embarrass you by picking you up. You can either walk home or get a ride with friends. But if anything like this ever happens again..."

"Oh, thanks, Daddy. You can trust us," said Beth.

"It won't!" softly but firmly said the boy.

Brad felt as though he had never loved them more nor been more proud of them.

The years passed too fast for Brad. The children, by now almost adults, had been his pride, his love, and his company.

By the end of their junior year, Brad had begun to dread the fact that in about a year they would be leaving for college and would no longer be with him full time. He hated the thought of being alone, but he wanted them to proceed to the next level of their lives without feeling sorry for him. Because of that, he tried his best not to show how he was feeling.

The summer found the twins again working, Brad in the asphalt plant and Beth at the swimming pool. Weekends found them busy with Beth working at the pool, and Brad running around with his friends or dating. Occasionally on Saturdays he would fish with his father, who, when not fishing with his son, was fishing with his friend, Allen.

Once during a lull in the fishing, Allen spoke up, "Brad," he said, "you are about the most forlorn guy I ever saw. What the hell is the matter with you? You don't kid around anymore. You can catch a big fish and not even get excited. You've told me about your lost love, but my God, man, get over it."

"That's not it, Allen. Truth is I'm dreading my kids growing up and going off to school. I know they need to go, and I know they are bound to grow up. I just hate to think of them leaving and my being alone. They have always been a great comfort to me."

"So that's it. Well, what can I say? They're going. Get over it. I know that's bullshit, but what else can you do? Why don't you start dating? There's a few single women around and a few younger widows, too. You can't grieve for the one that got away all your life."

" I know that, Allen. And I don't think I grieve for her. I just know I'll always love her, and you can't love two women at the same time. If you tried, the ghost of the first love would undermine the second and would be unfair to her. You know what happened to

Angela."

"Now cut out that crap. You didn't cause Angela to commit suicide. She was messed up in the head and maybe on dope to boot. Stop kicking yourself. Go out and find someone, get laid a bunch of times, and have fun."

"Allen, my mother once said you could marry for love or for lust, and she was right. I married for lust, and you saw where that led me. I'll not make that mistake again nor will I mislead some nice woman. I can only love once; I did, and I lost. Now go back to fishing and let it lie."

"My friend, I just hate to see you sad," was all Allen could say.

"I'll get over it," replied Brad. Just then a big bass took his bait and the fight was on, the discussion ended.

Summer ended, school started, and Brad, Jr. won the starting quarterback job on the Panther football team. Beth was a cheerleader.

On the first series of offensive plays, Brad took a hit on his right knee and fell to the ground in pain. His father and Don Glover examined him on the field, and both realized it was a serious injury. The MRI exam revealed a torn anterior cruciate ligament.

It was up to Brad to give his son the news. "Brad, you've got a torn ACL. You're gonna need surgery. I'm sorry, but your football days are over."

"I know it, Dad," he said through tears. "I knew it when I first felt it. I even heard it pop. Can it be fixed?"

"As good as new. You'll need extensive rehab, though."

"That's okay. I'll do it. I just hate there'll be no more football."

"Yeah, that's right, but you'll still be able to take all the pretty girls dancing when you get to the university. Don't forget that."

"I won't," said the boy.

The surgery was done at the Baptist Hospital in Little Rock. It was successful, and within ninety days Brad was walking without a limp.

"Mom," Brad said to Marian one evening when they were alone, "I need to ask you something."

"Go ahead, son."

"How did you feel when I left for college and even before I left? Were you bothered or sad or both?"

"Brad, I was both. In fact, I was downright depressed. I dreaded being alone because you were all I had after your dad died. Sometimes you were a pain in the rear, but most of the time you were a joy."

"I dreaded being alone, but I wanted you to get on with your life. After awhile, I got used to it. My job, my church and my friends helped."

"Mom, I feel the same way. You had a good marriage; I didn't. All I had was those two kids. They were a handful at times, but they were my joy. I'm going to miss them something awful, but I want them to go and get on with their lives. I just dread being alone."

"Honey, maybe you'll find some nice woman..."

"No, Mom," he said, slamming his fist into his other palm. "I've only been in love once, and that has been forever. It wouldn't be fair to another woman. You know that. I've told you many times."

"Well, honey, you'll survive," was all she could say.

In mid-October, Brad received a call from the police.

"Dr. Duncan," the officer said, "please come to the station. We have your son."

"What happened? What did he do?" Brad asked. "Was alcohol involved?"

"Nothing like that, Doc. Just come on down. We'll explain when you get here."

Brad threw on a scrub suit and hurried out the door just as his daughter drove up.

"All right, young lady, what's going on?"

"Aw, Daddy, we just pulled a stunt and some old lady called the cops. We all ran off, but Brad couldn't run because of the crutches."

"Get in the car. You can tell me all about it on the way to the jail."

"They've got Brad in jail?" she yelled.

"Calm down and get in the car," he said.

She did as she was told, and they started to town.

"All right. Let's have it," he said.

"We were at a party over at Molly's house. We were all standing around the piano singing. Molly's mom was playing the piano. After awhile she said, 'Why don't you all take Molly's doll out on the town and have some fun?'"

"What doll?" he asked.

"Molly's mom made her a life-sized doll and dressed her up like a woman. We thought it would be fun so we took it down to the school and laid it out by the curb so it looked like a car had hit it. The doll's head was next to where some car had leaked some oil. It looked like blood in the dark.

"Well, every once in a while a car would stop, and the driver would get out and run up to the doll. The he'd cuss and get back in the car and drive off.

"After a while a lady drove up with two little girls in the car. They stopped and held down on the horn. The little girls started screaming, and one of them yelled that someone had killed that poor woman."

Brad was trying hard not to laugh.

Beth went on, "Brad said we better stop and take the doll home, but then here came the police and an ambulance and a fire truck. We all took off running, but Brad couldn't run because of the crutches, so I guess they caught him."

"So you're gonna let your brother take the rap, are you?" Brad said.

"No sir. I'll confess, but I'm not gonna rat out on my friends."

When they got to the police station, there sat Brad holding his crutches.

The policeman said, "Doc, it was just a prank and kinda funny at that, but it upset some folks who had to make an emergency run. Your boy wasn't the only one. I bet that pretty little girl was in on it, too. Hell, I was a kid once. I'm gonna let him go this time, but if anything like this happens again, they better watch out. If I arrested this boy, I'd probably have to arrest half the school. Take him on home."

On the way home Brad said, "If I'm ever called to the police station about one of you again, you're in deep trouble." Then he laughed, and the twins finally relaxed.

The twins' senior year passed too fast for their father. Christmas came and went, and spring seemed to come too soon for Brad. Finally toward the end of May it was time for graduation, and Brad was trying his best not to reveal how sad he was. Marian tried without success to raise his spirits until finally she just gave up and said, "Get over it!"

Both Brad, Jr. and Beth had made very high scores on the SAT. Beth was valedictorian and her brother was fourth in the class. Grades and test scores were such that both the twins qualified for and were granted scholarships to the university in Fayetteville. Both planned to go into pre-med to become physicians.

During the graduation exercises, Brad, the senior class president, introduced his sister, the valedictorian. Beth stood straight, walked to the podium with a faint smile on her face and looked directly at her father. Then she grinned broadly and began her speech. Her father felt as though she was speaking directly to him. He was very proud of her and also of his son. After the ceremony, the three Duncans went to Marian's house for dinner.

During the meal their grandmother asked the twins how they planned to spend the summer.

Brad, Jr. was quiet and looked away, but Beth glanced at her father and then with some temerity said, "We've not told Daddy yet, but we've decided to go to summer school at the university. We can get twelve hours and be ahead when the fall semester begins. We want to have enough hours to get into med school after three years and maybe have enough hours at that time to even graduate early."

Marian glanced at her son and then said, "I think that's a great idea."

After a short pause Brad said, "I'll go along with that although I'm not ready for you to leave me yet. But I guess I'll live." They all laughed.

Knowing how their father dreaded their leaving, the kids had made all the arrangements for summer school prior to revealing their plans to him. Once he found out what they wanted to do he was supportive and did all he could to help them prepare to leave.

As the time drew near, he said to them, "Kiddos, you know I hate to see you leave. I'm gonna be lonely and will miss you very much. But I know you've got to grow up and prepare for a life of your own, and I want you to do it. I'm a big boy; I'll get over it. Maybe you can come back to Fabre's Bluff when you are doctors and practice with me, but I don't want you to do that if you want something else. Everyone has to march to his own drummer, and your drummer may not be the same as mine.

"So follow your drummer and do your own thing. Old Dad will support you whatever you decide."

Both his children hugged him and told him they loved him. All three had to choke back tears.

Too soon the day came. Brad wanted to go with them to help them get settled, but both said it was something they needed to do on their own, and Brad agreed.

For the summer the twins would take only the boy's car, which they would share. Beth would get her car in the fall when each planned to pledge one of the Greek organizations.

After hugs and a few tears from all three, Brad said, "Okay, kiddos, take off, study hard, have fun. Your old man is proud of you and loves you more than anything in the world. I'll see you in August."

As he watched the car go out of sight, Brad thought of his departing for college and was amazed at how fast the time had passed. He thought of how his mother must have felt about his leaving and how alone she must have felt. Knowing how he felt, he appreciated her even more.

He knew this day would come and thought he had prepared himself for it, but still was surprised how sad he was and how alone he felt. Thoughts of the twins' childhood flooded his mind. The memory of their mother rejecting them and then killing herself rekindled old stored-up anger. How anyone could not want to love and nurture such wonderful kids was beyond his understanding.

Finally he remembered his mother saying get over it, and he turned and entered his empty house.


The first few weeks of that summer were hard on Brad. He fished with his friend, Allen, on his afternoons off and even tried golf on Saturdays, but soon found that golf was not for him. All those he played with shot in the nineties, and he couldn't even get close to a hundred. Soon he realized golf was not for beginners in their forties.

On one very hot day in early July as he swung at his ball in the fairway, his club slipped out of his hand and landed about twenty feet up in a tree. All four of his group threw golf balls at the club until finally one dislodged it, and it fell to the ground.

"That's it," said Brad, as he put the club back in his bag. "If someone would give me a couple of hundred dollars, I'd sell these damned clubs!"

Allen said, "I'll give you two hundred," and took two one hundred dollar bills from his pocket.

Brad took the money and handed his friend the bag of clubs. Then he asked, "What size shoes do you wear?"

"Eleven and a half," replied Allen.

"Can you wear twelves?" Brad asked.

"Sure," replied Allen.

Brad sat on the ground, took off his golf shoes, handed them to Allen, and said, "Here's a present."

He took off his socks, put them in his pocket, bid farewell and walked off the course in his bare feet, vowing never to step on a golf course again.

At the clinic the next Monday, Don Glover entered Brad's main office, closed the door, and sat down. "Brad" he said, "I know you are lonely. I know you miss your kids. You need to have some sort of a social life. My cousin, Rosemary Jones, has moved to El Dorado. Rosie is attractive, ten years younger than you, and recently divorced. I won't go into the reasons for the divorce except to say that Rosie wasn't at fault.

"She has been hurt, too hurt for someone as nice as she is. Now I'm not trying to be a matchmaker. She sure is not ready for a serious relationship, but she does need someone to know, to be able to talk to and do things with. You need the same thing. That's why I think you would be good for each other."

Brad tried to resist.

"I'm not taking no for an answer," said Don. "MaryAnn and I have invited her to dinner at the house Saturday night. I'm inviting you, and I insist on your accepting."

Brad knew he needed to do something to get out of his funk, so he accepted. The entire week he worried about it. What if she wanted to get serious, he thought. But in the end he decided to give it a try, even though he had no intention of ever being romantically attached to another woman again. Beth was still, and would always be, the sole occupant of his heart.

Saturday night came too soon, and Brad knocked on the Glovers' door at precisely seven o'clock. Don answered the door and, after exchanging pleasantries, led his friend into the den.

MaryAnn arose and gave Brad a hug. Then Don said, "Rosie, this is my friend and partner, Brad Duncan. Brad, this is my cousin, Rosemary Jones, but everyone calls her Rosie."

"Hi, Brad," said Rosemary.

"Hi, Rosie, it's good to meet you. Cousin Don had spoken very highly of you, but he hasn't done you justice."

Rosemary blushed and then said, "Why Brad, you're not flirting with me already, are you?"

Then it was Brad's turn to blush, and the Glovers both laughed. Rosemary reminded him of Beth, not so much in looks but by her fresh sense of humor. He decided that maybe he could enjoy her company.

As the summer progressed, Brad began to see Rosemary often, although always in a platonic sense. He enjoyed her company but had no romantic or sensual urges toward her. She enjoyed crappie fishing so many afternoons were spent on small river lakes. Often when their luck was good, Rosemary would cook their daily catch at her home in El Dorado. Brad enjoyed those meals with her but always left for home early.

Finally in late July, after six weeks of their relationship, Rosemary brought up the subject Brad was dreading.

"Brad," she said after they finished an evening meal, "we've been seeing each other quite a lot this summer. You've hugged me a time or two, but you've never kissed me. I think we've had enough time together that I have a right to know what your intentions are toward me."

"Rosie, I don't know what to say. You are very nice and quite attractive, and I enjoy being with you a lot. We've had great times together," he replied.

"You know that's not what I mean. What are your feelings toward me? Do you see any future for us?"

"Well, I owe you honesty," he said, and she began to pull away in anticipation of what she felt was coming next. "I have been in love. It ended badly, and I was hurt beyond description. Something must be wrong with me, but I just cannot feel love in a romantic sense. Platonically yes, but love, as a man should feel for a woman, no. I treasure your friendship, but it would be unfair to you or to any woman to try to go farther than that."

She looked away, was silent for a while, and then said, "Brad, I want more than that, and remaining as we are will ultimately become too painful for me. So let's just break this relationship off right now. I can see you loved your wife very much."

He got up to leave, they shook hands, and as he opened the door he turned back and said, "It wasn't my wife." Then he left.

A s the summer went on, Brad was both lonely and bored. He thought he detected a change in Don's attitude toward him but finally he decided it was just his guilty conscience.

The days passed fast since he was quite busy, but the nights and weekends when he wasn't on call were quite lonely. On Saturdays he would fish alone and then grab a sandwich at night and settle down to a book or television.

Sundays were spent in church and then noon dinner at his mother's. They had little to talk about, so as soon as he felt it was proper, he excused himself and left. Those afternoons he would go for long walks or take trips through the countryside by car. During those times Beth was on his mind. Where did she live, was she happy, did she have a good marriage, did she have children? Those unanswerable questions haunted him always.

There was a small hidden cove on the river bank that he felt was his private sanctuary. He felt close to God there. He would tell God his problems and hope for answers.

One Sunday afternoon, on a hot August day, he found his way there. After pouring out his soul to God, he asked, "Will this hurt, this torment, about Beth ever leave me? I wish you could answer me or at least give me a sign."

As he looked up he saw two ducks, a mallard drake and a hen, flying from around the river's bend at eye level with him and down the river and out of his sight. When they were even with him, they seemed to look toward him. Migratory ducks were not supposed to be in the area that time of year.

Brad took that as a sign in answer to his request and left the river with peace of mind that had eluded him for years.

In late August the twins came home for a ten day break prior to starting the fall semester. Brad was delighted to have them, but they seemed changed—more grown up; more sophisticated.

They brought him up on all they had seen and done during the summer session, but then they were ready to see all their friends and spend time with them. Brad was pleased for them but was disappointed that they didn't want to spend more time with him.

Over dinner at Marian's house the third night they were home, the twins told Brad and his mother all about school in particular and Fayetteville in general.

Beth said, "Some of the Pi Phis have been rushing me pretty hard. I really like them , and unless one of the other sororities rushes me strong, I plan to pledge Pi Phi. I love their house, and the girls are real nice and lots of fun."

"How about you, young man?" Marian asked Brad, Jr.

"Kappa Sig all the way," replied Brad.

"What was good for your dad will do for you, eh?" she replied.

"It's a great frat, and many of my friends and a lot of guys I know from other towns belong. I know I'll like it better than the rest although the Skis are good."

"What in the world are Skis?" asked Marian.

"That's slang for Sigma Chi, Mom. Looks like my Brad has become Joe College in just two months," said Brad, Sr.

They all laughed, and young Brad just blushed.

The time passed too fast, and the kids were getting ready to leave. As Brad watched each of his children pack their cars, it was obvious he was sad, although he was trying not to show it.

"Don't be sad, Daddy. You can come up to all the football games and see us, and we'll be home Thanksgiving. Tell Etta Mae we want a sweet potato pie for sure," said Beth.

"Dad," said Brad, "we heard talk about you and some lady Dr. Glover fixed you up with. She can keep you company. Maybe something will come of it even though you never told us about her."

"That was brief and is over," Brad replied.

The twins accepted that and got in their separate cars.

"You kids drive within eyesight of each other and be careful. I love you."

"We'll be careful. We love you, too," they both said.

"We'll see you at the first game," yelled Beth, as they pulled out of the driveway.

Brad watched sadly as the taillights disappeared and then went into his empty house.

The six hour trip to Fayetteville was uneventful for the twins. They did as they were told and kept within sight of each other with Beth leading the way. Both were looking forward to rush week and the start of school, but thoughts of their father being so lonely bothered them both. They each vowed to write frequently and phone often. They needn't worry about housekeeping or meals since he still had Etta Mae.

It was dark when they arrived at the apartment they had shared for the summer session. They each unpacked, had a sandwich, and retired to their respective rooms.

Rush began the next day and lasted a week. To the satisfaction of both, Beth received a bid from Pi Phi and Brad from Kappa Sigma.

Both accepted, closed the apartment, and moved into their respective Greek houses. It was the first time in their lives that they hadn't lived together.

After a weekend of getting to know their housemates and settling in, they met each other at registration. Comparing their schedules they found they only had one class together—freshman English. They were pleased they had only one class together, because each felt the need to develop an identity unrelated to the other. Each had always been identified as the other's twin, and each needed his or her own unique identity.

The first day of classes found the twins together in English class at eight o'clock. Brad took care to take a seat as far away from Beth as he could.

At precisely eight the door opened, and an attractive woman who appeared to be in her early forties entered. She was of above average height, slender but well formed, with moderate brown short-cropped hair and dark brown eyes.

She stood beside her desk, smiled at the class, asked for quiet and began to speak.

"I address you as men and women since you are now considered grown and no longer boys and girls. I'm sure you have noticed the dormitories are named men's dorms and women's dorms. That means you are expected by this school to act as adults. I expect no less of you.

"My name is Elizabeth Collins. You may call me Miss Collins since I have never been married, and I detest the term Miz. Now for some of you hiding a snicker I am not a lesbian. You may think of me as an old maid if you wish since I am just a little north of forty.

"We are going to use proper grammar in this class. If you use improper grammar, even in casual conversation, and I hear it, I will grade you down. You can depend on that, particularly if the improper grammar is one of my pet peeves.

"What are my pet peeves? One is 'where it's at'. I know that has become so commonly used to be almost acceptable, but it is not acceptable to me. The proper term is 'where it is'.

"I will not tolerate the non-word 'ain't'. Someone once said, 'Ain't ain't a word'."

That brought about laughs from the students.

"Well, it isn't a word but rather a colloquialism. So don't say ain't.

"My pet peeve, and the one that makes my skin crawl, is the improper use of the plural when speaking of two people. 'He gave it to Mary and I' drives me crazy. Would you say 'he gave it to I'? Of course not. You would say 'he gave it to me'. So the proper plural expression is 'he gave it to Mary and me'. Just think of how it sounds in the singular before you say it in the plural. 'I' is the subjective form, and 'me' is the objective form.

"Any questions? No? Then let's get to work. I do want to say this. I expect you to be responsible and attend class; however, I will not take roll. If you can miss all the class sessions and then still pass my tests, that is alright with me, but I'll bet you can't. If you get a bad grade, don't come whining and begging to me. I will not change a grade for anyone. I expect you to be responsible adults.

"All right. Open your books to page one, and let's get started."

On Friday of the first week, Miss Collins dismissed the class fifteen minutes early. As the students got up to leave she said, "Would Miss Duncan and Mr. Duncan wait a few minutes?"

When Beth and Brad approached her desk, Miss Collins said, "Brother and sister, man and wife, or no relation?"

"We're twins, unfortunately," said Beth.

Brad just nodded.

"A sense of humor; I like that," said the teacher. "Where are you from?"

Brad spoke up, "We're from Fabre's Bluff in south Arkansas."

"Isn't that close to El Dorado?"

"Yes ma'am," said Beth.

"Tell me about yourselves. Do you like being twins?"

"It's okay," said Beth. "We get along okay, but Brad goes his way, and I go mine. Our father always encouraged us to develop our own identities. Brad likes sports, and I lean more to the arts. Brad is great in math, and I had to work hard to get an A."

"What does your father do for a living?"

"He's a doctor," said Brad. "That's one of the reasons we're in pre-med. Both of us want to be doctors and, unless we change our minds later, go back to Fabre's Bluff and practice with him."

"Tell me about your mother."

Brad and Beth looked at each other, and then Beth said, "She's dead."

"Oh, I'm sorry," said Elizabeth.

"That's okay," said Brad. "She died when we were three. We barely remember her."

"Well, thanks," said Elizabeth. "You can leave now. I was just wondering if you were married or siblings."

As they walked down the hall, Beth said, "What was all that about?"

"Damned if I know," replied Brad.

A few days later Beth was in the campus library researching for a paper due in her Western Civilization class. She was alone at a corner desk using her laptop when she noticed Miss Collins coming toward her.

"Hello, Miss Duncan. How are you?"

"I'm fine, Miss Collins. How are you?"

"For a newcomer to Fayetteville and the U of A, I'm doing well. I've about finished getting squared away in my apartment. May I sit with you for a minute?"

"Of course," said Beth.

.

For a while they sat in silence, and then Elizabeth spoke up. "I'll bet your full name is Elizabeth like mine," she said.

"No ma'am. Beth is my real given name. Once I asked Daddy why Brad had a dignified name like Bradley Andrew, Jr., and I was just plain Beth. He said he liked Beth and that was that."

"Well, Beth is a pretty name, and it goes well with Brad. It seems very appropriate since you are twins. Was your mother's name Beth?"

"No ma'am. Her name was Angela."

"I'll bet she was pretty to give birth to a young woman as beautiful as you."

"She was attractive. I've seen photos of her but no portraits. My father never talks of her so Brad and I know little of her."

Elizabeth was quiet for a moment and then said, "It is so sad that she died when you were so young. My mother died when I was a teenager, and I still miss her. Please pardon me for prying, but would you mind telling me what she died of? That is if you care to talk about it."

Beth was quiet, so Elizabeth spoke up, "I'm sorry, Beth, I shouldn't have asked. Please forgive me."

"That's okay, Miss Collins. She committed suicide. Daddy told us she just got sick and couldn't get well, but kids in grammar school told us she killed herself. Brad and I asked Nanny about it when we were teenagers, and she told us the whole story. She said our mother was depressed for a long time and had abused drugs. She was a nurse and got caught diverting drugs meant for her patients. She lost her job and just decided to end it. She overdosed on drugs no one knew she had. We never told Daddy we knew."

"Beth, I am so sorry I asked," was all Elizabeth could say.

"That's okay, Miss Collins. Neither Brad nor I is bothered by it. We can't remember her ever even holding us. Nanny, our grandmother, finally told us that she was so sick she couldn't care for anyone but herself. Our father was both father and mother to us. He raised us with help from Nanny and Etta Mae, our housekeeper. Daddy even gave up delivering babies, which he loved, so he wouldn't have to leave us at night."

"Your father must be a wonderful man," said Elizabeth.

"He sure is," said Beth.

Later when Beth told Brad about her conversation with Miss Collins, Brad said, "Dammit Beth, why did you have to tell her all that?"

"I don't know. She just seemed so sincere and really cared about us. I felt so comfortable with her."

Six weeks passed routinely for fall semesters. There were three football victories and one loss. Only two of the games had been played in Fayetteville, both attended by the twins, each with a date. Their father could not come to either of those two home games due to his call schedule. He did see the Little Rock game and enjoyed dinner at Bruno's with the twins, neither of whom had dates.

During the meal each brought their father up to date on school, and he told them what was going on at the Bluff, particularly with Marian and Etta Mae.

"What about your classes?" he asked. "I hope you're both making good grades."

"We're doing fine," said Beth. Her brother nodded.

"What courses do you like best?"

"Daddy, you're not going to believe this, but it's English. We've got the neatest teacher."

"Yeah," broke in Brad, "but she's gonna be tough and a hard A for sure."

"How's that?" asked their father.

"Well," the son said, "she's a stickler for proper grammar for one thing. If you say 'you and I' when you should have said 'you and me', she knocks off on your grade, and you better not say 'where it's at'."

Brad, Sr. grinned. "Well, good for her," he said.

"But she's real nice," said Beth.

"She is nice," said Brad, Jr., "but she's a little flaky I think. The first day she told us she was an old maid and to address her as Miss Collins and not Miz Collins. She made sure to point out she was not a lesbian, too."

"Sounds like someone I'd like to meet. I'll be up there for the Auburn game in two weeks. I'll be at the Hilton and will get there in the early afternoon. If the Venetian Inn is still there in Tontitown, that's where I'd like to take you Friday night."

"It's there," said Brad, "but we haven't eaten there."

"Good. It's set then, the Venetian Inn for sure. I used to eat there on Sunday nights with a girl I was dating. If you have dates, they are welcome to go with us."

The Auburn weekend finally came, and as he promised, Brad checked into the Hilton around two that Friday.

He had hardly settled into his room when the twins showed up.

"Come on, Daddy, we want to show you the homecoming decorations," said Beth. "Ours is good, but the Kappa Sigs have stolen the show."

As they drove down Dickson Street, Brad, Sr. said, "Let's park the car at the Kappa Sig house and walk over the campus."

The twins agreed, and Beth said, "We can look for your name on the sidewalk. I haven't been able to find it."

"That's because it isn't there. I left here for med school after my junior year. My name's on a plaque in the basement of the med school."

As the three were walking down one of the senior walks, Beth said, "Here comes Miss Collins."

As they neared her, Brad could hardly believe his eyes. "Beth!" he shouted.

"What?" said his daughter.

"He wasn't talking to you," said her brother.

"Hi, Brad. I knew these were your kids. They both look a lot like I remember you."

She held out her hand to shake with him. He took her hand and pulled her to him and hugged her. She did not resist.

The twins were shocked, and his daughter thought she saw a tear in her father's eye.

The twins went back to the hotel with their dad. Brad had invited Beth to have dinner with him and the kids at the Venetian Inn. She had accepted and would meet them in the hotel lobby at six.

They made the trip to the hotel in silence. Brad was in deep thought, and the twins were confused.

When they arrived at the hotel, Brad said, "Kiddos, come up to the room with me. I've got some explaining to do."

When they reached Brad's room, the twins sat on a couch, and Brad sat on the edge of the bed. "Beth, Miss Collins, and I met at Hardy when we were eleven. Well, she was almost eleven. We spent a day together, and it was a most wonderful day – almost magical. We were to spend the next day together, but when I went to her cabin, she and her parents had gone.

"I had no idea where she lived. I tried to find out from the resort manager, but he wouldn't give me any information. I was distraught for, believe it or not, I had fallen in love with her even at that young age.

"I never got over her. I looked for her everywhere, but had no luck. All through high school I dated some, but I never got Beth out of my mind."

"Daddy," his Beth said, "you named me after her, didn't you?"

"Yes, honey, I did."

"Well, why didn't you name me Elizabeth like her?"

"Because her name wasn't Elizabeth. It was Beth. I remember her telling me that when she grew up she was going to hire a lawyer and change her name to Elizabeth Anne with an e. I guess she did.

"Anyway, we met again our sophomore year here in Fayetteville. We found that we both felt the same way, and we fell in love all over again. But there was a misunderstanding and she left. She thought I had been unfaithful to her, and I had not."

He felt he had said enough so he tried to finish the explanation. "I couldn't find where she went. It doesn't matter what the misunderstanding was – it was neither my fault nor hers, but we were through. I will admit that I never got over her."

"Dad," said his son, "did you ever really love our mother?"

"I thought I did. I tried to. I did care for her, but love? Not like I felt for Beth."

"Did she know about Miss Collins?" asked Beth.

"No. No one knew about her except for your grandmother. I was good to your mother and tried to be a good husband, but she was too sick to care."

"I know," said Beth. "She killed herself."

"How did you know that?" Brad asked.

Brad, Jr. spoke up. "Kids in school. We finally asked Nanny, and she admitted it was true. She told us she was mentally ill and none of it was our fault. Dad, you've been, and are, a wonderful father and we love you very much."

Brad went to them, and all three embraced.

Finally Beth said, "Daddy, we need to get out of here and let you and Miss Collins be alone together. Come on, Brad, let's get out of here."

They left, and their father didn't protest.

At five-thirty, Brad went down to the lobby, and Beth was sitting on a couch waiting for him.

"Where are your kids?" she asked.

"They felt we should be alone together to discuss old times. I didn't argue with them. In fact, I was trying to figure out a way to get rid of them."

"That wasn't very nice," she said with a straight face. He wasn't sure whether she was teasing until she laughed. The same Beth, he thought. What a sense of humor.

"Where's your car?" he asked.

"I only live a few blocks from here. I walked."

"Good," he said. "When I take you home I'll get to see where you live. Maybe you'll invite me in."

Now he could tell she was serious. "That depends, Brad. We have a lot to talk about before we get to that point. There's been a lot of water under the bridge in the last twenty-eight years."

He said no more but walked her to his car and opened the door for her.

"Wow," she said, "A Beemer and a 750LI too. Small town doctoring must be quite rewarding."

That embarrassed him, but he replied, "It's my one indulgence. I couldn't resist it. At home I drive a Chevy truck. You see, my kids are pretty smart and have scholarship money, and also I've been saving for their college all their lives. I have almost no expenses, an ordinary paid-for house, and only myself and my kids to support."

They drove on in silence. He had many questions, but he didn't want to ask them while driving.

They arrived at the Venetian Inn at their appointed time. Brad requested and was given a secluded table.

"The same old Venetian Inn," she said, after they were seated. "This is my first time here since returning to Fayetteville."

They had nothing other than small talk while they ate their steaks. Neither wanted wine. Finally over coffee Beth broke the ice.

"Tell me about your wife," she said.

"Beth, that's a helluva way to start a conversation that I really want to have with you, but here goes.

"Angela was a registered nurse. We knew each other casually in school. We had classes together. After I lost you I was lonely, and frankly I was broken-hearted. Anyway, we started dating a little after I lost you, and then seriously after I got in med school.

"Mom had met her and didn't really like her. She told me I was in lust and not in love. I didn't really believe that. I thought I was just lonely. You were gone. I couldn't find you, and then when I found out you were married, I just gave up."

Beth looked surprised but only said, "Go on."

"Well, I guess Angie saw me as a gravy train. She tricked me into marriage by telling me she was pregnant. She wasn't, but I didn't find out until much later. Mom suspected it first, but Angie just said she had miscarried.

"Time passed. She got pregnant with the twins and hated me for it. She wanted an abortion, but I refused and threatened to divorce her if she got one. When the babies came, she refused to hold them or even name them. She said they were my babies, and it was up to me to take care of them.

"I had, and still have, a wonderful colored woman named Etta Mae who helped me raise them. Mom helped too.

"Angie got caught diverting drugs for her own use, lost her job, and was going to lose her nurse's license.

"When the kids were three she killed herself. I'll admit I was relieved. I've been both mother and father to Beth and Brad."

"You love them very much, don't you?" Beth said.

"Beth, I adore them. They've been my whole life. I'm lonesome without them. God, I hated to see them leave for college."

"You named Beth after me, didn't you?"

"Of course I did; but now it's your turn. Tell me about your life, your husband, and all."

"I never married. I never had more than casual dates."

"What? But Marie told me you had married."

"Then she lied. Whatever happened to her?"

"Killed in a car wreck my junior year. She was drunk."

"Okay Brad. Tell me about the girl you got pregnant in Fayetteville. I saw you put her on a bus."

"I know," he said, "Marie told me. Beth, that was my cousin. Abigail was a secretary for a lawyer in Fayetteville. She got pregnant and came to me for help. I got her in the Florence Crittenton Home in Little Rock. I was putting her on the bus for Little Rock when you saw me. She had the baby and gave it up for adoption. I've seen her only rarely since then."

"But Marie told me..."

He interrupted her, "Beth, I don't know why but Marie wanted to get together with me. I liked her and trusted her, but I wasn't interested in any romance with her. I guess she would have done anything.

"She told me you were married. Before that, when she sent my letter to you, she told me you said you didn't believe me and never wanted to see me again."

"She never sent me a letter from you. She didn't even know where I was. I never wrote her; I never phoned her. The last time I saw her was the day I saw you at the bus with that girl. I just told her I was leaving, and I left. That was all."

"Tell me about your life," he said.

"I went back to Fulton and stayed with my grandparents for about six months. She died suddenly, and he just dried up. Eight days later he died.

"I settled their estate over the next six months. I was their only heir, and they left everything to me that they didn't leave to their church.

"I moved to Colorado and enrolled in Colorado U. I had plenty of money so I stayed through my master's then got a job teaching English at the university. Over the next couple of years I taught and got my doctorate. So you see, I'm a doctor, too—a doctor of education.

"I taught there until five years ago. I got breast cancer and had a pretty rough time. I had a lumpectomy and then radiation, but now I'm okay. After that scare I just wanted to come home. I was happiest and then saddest here in Fayetteville at the university, so I applied here and was accepted.

"And wouldn't you know it, I had your kids in my first class."

"Are you sure the cancer is gone?"

"I've had a clean bill of health every time I've been checked. I had a full workup this past summer. The doctor said my long-term prognosis is excellent."

"Thank God," he said. "I see you did what you said you were going to do years ago in Hardy."

"What's that?"

"You legally changed your name. I'll bet it was changed to Elizabeth Anne with an e."

"It was; it is."

The drive back to Fayetteville was over quickly. He walked her to the door of her little house and said, "Beth, I've loved you since we were eleven. I've never stopped loving you even when I was married. I'll never stop loving you. I want you to know that."

"Brad, I'm not going to invite you in. We both need to take a step back and think about this. Go back to your kids and enjoy your time with them. We'll see where this leads."

As he entered Saint Paul's Church in Fayetteville on that warm June day, he thought of how fast the past eight months had gone. So much had happened.

He looked around the empty sanctuary with its dark walls and vaulted ceiling, feeling finally at peace. He noticed the beautiful stained glass windows. In each window sill was a bouquet of red roses which he remembered were Beth's favorites.

He was early, but he felt the need to be there by himself before the service started. There were so many memories, and he wanted to nurture them all.

As he walked down the center aisle, he was met by the priest, Father Lawrence. "You're early, Doctor. Why don't you wait in my study?"

"Thank you, Father. I'll do that if you're sure it's okay."

"Of course it is," said the priest, as he guided Brad into the darkly paneled room with its leather couch and easy chairs.

He had rested in one of the chairs and was about to drift off when the twins came in. His son said, "Come on, Dad. It's time."

As he entered the chancel with his children and the priest, he was surprised to see so many people there, many of whom he hadn't seen in years. The size of the congregation almost moved him to tears. He followed Father Lawrence to the altar and stood beside him.

The afternoon sun through the narthex window was intensely lighting the center aisle so that when she stepped into view he was reminded of that afternoon so many years ago—that afternoon she was backlit by the sun as she came down the hillside path.

She stepped beside him, and he took her hand. When he heard the priest begin, "Dearly beloved, we are gathered together in the sight of God and this company here present to join together this man and this woman . . . " Brad felt Beth squeeze his hand three times.